My Easter Basket
Stories, Songs, Poems, Recipes, Crafts, and Fun for Kids

Sheri Brownrigg

Illustrations By Mary Collier • Photographs By David Hughes

SMITHMARK

Contents

Introduction 5

CHAPTER ONE
Spring Brings Easter 6
Spring Pasta 10
The Boy Who Discovered the Spring 11
Butterfly Card 16

CHAPTER TWO
Parades and Bonnets 18
Party Smoothies 21
Secrets at the Mardi Gras 22
Your Own Easter Bonnet 26

CHAPTER THREE
Here Comes the Easter Bunny 28
Gingerbread Bunnies 31
Alice in Easterland 32
Kachina Rabbit 36

CHAPTER FOUR
Easter Baskets, Toys, and Treats 38
Marzipan Chicks 41
Abbott's Habit 42
Patchwork Basket 46

CHAPTER FIVE
Baby Easter Animals 48
Baby Lettuce Salad 51
Easter Lamb 52
Mechanical Chickadee 56

CHAPTER SIX
A Dozen Eggs 58
Egg in the Eye with Green
Tomato Salsa 61
Eric's Excellent Easter Adventure 62
Egg Globe 66

CHAPTER SEVEN
Fun Buns 68
Pretzels 71
Elena's Ciambella 72
Bread Dough Dove 76

CHAPTER EIGHT
Flower Power 78
Antipasto Flowers 81
The Magic Easter Lily 82
Foam-Lily 85

Index 87

Introduction

IN THE SAME WAY THAT THE BASKET THE EASTER BUNNY BRINGS IS FULL OF goodies, *My Easter Basket* is packed full of tales, treats, crafts, and fun. Discover why Easter is celebrated and how it ties into other spring festivals. How did the Easter Bunny start delivering eggs? And why do eggs have such a big part in the holiday? Who started decorating eggs so beautifully? *My Easter Basket* answers these questions and many more.

Eight wonderful stories, both realistic and fantastic, bring the Easter season to life. Have an adventure with Victor and Emile at the Mardi Gras parade, follow Alice down the White Rabbit's hole, and ride with Eric and the Easter Bunny in the Cosmic Egg as they deliver Easter goodies to children all over the world.

Craft and recipe ideas to help you celebrate the fun-filled Easter season are also included. Spring Pasta with curly noodles and spring vegetables, fanciful edible spring flower bouquets, and Egg in the Eye with Green Tomato Salsa are just a few of the delicious Easter treats you can make. The crafts include a silly Easter bonnet, a Patchwork Basket, a Kachina Rabbit, and a beautiful Easter lily.

As Easter draws closer, while you are waiting for the Easter Bunny to arrive, and all through the year, you will enjoy the goodies, adventure, and fun in *My Easter Basket*.

CHAPTER ONE

Spring Brings Easter

Flowers poke their heads above ground. Trees get new buds, and sunshine melts the snow and warms the brooks' cold water. Bears and other animals crawl out of their sleepy winter burrows. Caterpillars make their cocoons and start their journeys to becoming butterflies. Robins begin building their nests. All these are signs that, at last, it is spring!

On March 21 in North America, the earth tips on its axis so that the sun is directly over its middle, called the equator (e-KWAY-tor). We have a day that is equally divided between light and dark. Called the spring, or vernal, equinox (E-kwi-nox), this day marks the end of winter. Finally, it is spring, which also means that Easter is just around the corner.

Easter falls on the Sunday after the first full moon on or following March 21, the spring equinox. Easter is the most important holiday for Christians because it celebrates Jesus' resurrection about two thousand years ago.

Once the date of Easter is set, we count back to set the date for Lent, as well as the dates for Shrove Tuesday, Ash Wednesday, Palm Sunday, and the Holy Week just before Easter. These are all religious holidays that commemorate the time of Jesus' death and his Resurrection.

Even before Easter was celebrated, people celebrated spring in many different ways. In some places, since the people didn't understand how the seasons changed, they thought that a powerful god or goddess made the season's changes occur. Many of their beliefs and traditions have been carried into the celebration of Easter.

The ancient Greeks, for example, believed Demeter (di-MEET-er), the goddess of the earth and farming, caused spring to come each year. When Demeter's daughter Persephone (per-

Beautiful Spring Days

On beautiful Spring days
You see gleaming lakes,
With nameless ducks quacking
The mighty wind blowing,
Squirrels scatting from tree to tree,
Birds vanishing in the cloud,
Flowers opening their petals gracefully,
Kites flying freely in the blueish sky,
The gleaming sun trying to push
The clouds out of its way.
Sap going down my throat
The gaunt dark bark from the trees
Tomorrow will be a new Spring day.

— Jonathan Garber

Countdown to Easter

Although the Easter Bunny comes on one day, the Easter season starts several weeks before. Starting with Mardi Gras, the party right before the quiet time of Lent, this time helps you prepare for the glorious day of Easter itself and to celebrate the coming of spring.

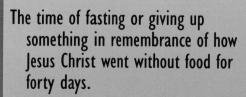

Pre-Lent

Carnival: a time of feasting and merry-making celebrated just before the start of the forty days of Lent.

Shrovetide: the last three or four days before Lent begins.

Mardi Gras: the principal celebration of Carnival. Mardi Gras means "Fat Tuesday" in French. Celebrations with parades and parties are held in many parts of the world. Mardi Gras is always on the Tuesday forty days before Easter.

Lent

The time of fasting or giving up something in remembrance of how Jesus Christ went without food for forty days.

Ash Wednesday: the beginning of the forty-day fast. Church ceremonies remind people that they should observe Lent as a time of quiet.

SEF-uh-nee) was kidnapped by the god Hades (HEY-dees), king of the underworld, Demeter was so sad that she let all the plants on Earth wither and die. Finally, Zeus (zoose), king of all the gods, let Persephone come back to Earth for six months every year. When Persephone returned, Demeter brought all the plants and animals back to life.

In northern and central parts of Europe, children believed in the goddess of spring called Eostre (es-TRAY). Every year they would welcome Eostre's return by baking special cakes and honoring her with a festival. It is believed that the word "Easter" came from this goddess' name.

The Celts (kelts), who lived in Great Britain in ancient times, believed their sun god was thrown in a great dark prison for part of the year by evil spirits of cold and darkness. So, at the end of each winter, the Celts lit giant bonfires on the highest hills of their villages. They believed that the flames from these fires leaped up and crackled and frightened the evil spirits, forcing them to release the sun god.

Long ago, in Germany, the villagers believed that evil witches flew up to the mountains every spring, tormenting any little children they found along the way. So the villagers lit fires, blew horns, and made as much noise as they could to frighten away the evil spirits.

One of the most popular spring events in Japan is picnicking among the cherry blossoms in early April. Day to day, everyone spreads the news about where the best spot for cherry blossom viewing is.

The ancient spring festival of Vietnam is called Tet. This is short for Tet Nhat (TET naht), which means "the first day of the return of spring." The Vietnamese traditionally make new clothes, paint their homes and shops, and decorate their courtyards for the holiday, which lasts three days. On the last day of Tet, the unicorn comes dancing down the street. The unicorn, a mythical, horselike animal with one horn in the center of its forehead, is believed to bring good fortune and good crops in the coming year. The people follow her, dancing, singing, and lighting fireworks.

In India, there is a spring festival called Holi (HOH-lee), a holiday filled with music, dance, fire, water, and color. Young people collect scrap wood for a bonfire called the Holi Festival Fire. This fire burns all night long while people stand around it singing and dancing and playing the drums. When the sun comes up, the revelers pour water on the fire. They mark their faces with the ashes from the fire for good luck. This part of the rejoicing is a farewell to the old. Then they welcome the new season with a very unusual splattering of color. Children run through the streets carrying spray guns filled with brightly colored dyes or powders. They spray color on anything that moves, causing a joyful mess. Luckily, they have harmless dyes and powders that are specially made just for this occasion.

Chalanda Marz (CHA-lan-da MARS) is a Swiss celebration welcoming spring. On March 1, children wear cowbells around their waists or necks and go from house to house in groups, singing folk songs and ringing their bells. The people in the houses give them candy or money.

May Day is celebrated today in many places throughout the world. This celebration goes back to the time of Flora, the early Roman goddess of flowers and spring. Children attached brightly colored ribbons and flowers to the top of a tree or a pole, then wove the ribbons in an elaborate pattern down the pole in a dance to celebrate the arrival of spring. This was called the maypole dance. This dance is very beautiful, and it is still done in many places.

Easter celebrations have gone beyond Easter Sunday. In some places in northern England on the Monday and Tuesday following Easter Sunday, men and women used to play a game called "heaving" or "lifting." On Easter Monday, women would surround any man they met in the street and "heave" him over their heads three times. Then they would sprinkle him with water and each would give him a kiss. The next day it was the men's turn to "heave" the women they met on the street. Some forms of this game are still played today.

There are many different ways to celebrate spring and Easter. Both words mean "beginning again." But even without these traditions we can tell what time of year it is. New flowers tell our noses and baby birds sing to our ears that the year's new life is just ahead. Go ahead, celebrate! Spring brings Easter!

A Cherry Blossom Festival that includes parades and parties is held in Washington, D.C., every year at the beginning of April. The cherry trees were given to the United States in 1910 and 1912 as a gift of friendship by the mayor of Tokyo, Japan.

An Easter game called "switching" still takes place in some countries. In Poland, for instance, friends who meet tap each other lightly with a switch made from a bush stem. The tap is a reminder of Christ's sufferings during Holy Week and stands for a wish for purity.

Holy Week

The final week of Lent. Some churches hold special services on every day of this week. Holy Week recalls the events leading to Jesus' death and Resurrection.

Palm Sunday: the first day of Holy Week. This is the day of the Blessing of the Palms.

Maundy Thursday (Holy Thursday): This day recalls Jesus' last meal and His arrest.

Good Friday: observes the death of Jesus.

Holy Saturday: The Lenten fast ends at noon. In evening church services, congregations light candles and read the Easter story from the Bible.

Easter

The center of an entire season of the Christian year.

Easter Sunday: celebrates the Resurrection of Jesus. This day is for feasting and celebration.

Ascension Day: For forty days after Easter Sunday, Christians celebrate the time when Jesus reappeared to some of His followers. This period ends on Ascension Day, or Ascension Thursday.

Other Springtime Dates

March 21: The first day of Spring

May 1: May Day

Spring Pasta

Do you know the name for the pasta that's curled like a spring? It is called rotini. But in celebration of the season of Easter, let's call it Spring Pasta.

INGREDIENTS FOR 10 ½-CUP SERVINGS

1 bunch broccoli

1 red bell pepper

1 green bell pepper

1 12-oz. package three-color Spring Pasta (rotini)

Italian Dressing (see below)

1 cup chopped basil leaves

¼ cup chopped parsley

2 cloves garlic, crushed

½ cup grated Parmesan cheese

INGREDIENTS FOR ITALIAN DRESSING

2 tablespoons salad oil

2 tablespoons water

1 tablespoon red wine vinegar

1 teaspoon sugar

pinch of pepper

pinch of dry mustard

pinch of paprika

1. Wash broccoli and cut the florets from the stems. Pull the florets apart, making smaller bite-size pieces.

2. Bring about 2 cups of water to a boil in a saucepan and add broccoli florets. Bring to a boil again.

3. Lower heat, cover pan, and cook broccoli for about 10 minutes.

4. Drain broccoli in a colander and set aside.

5. Wash red and green peppers. Cut each in half, and clean the seeds out of the middle. Slice the 4 sections in half and then in half again. Chop these into pieces ¼ inch by ¼ inch. Set aside.

6. Bring 4 quarts of water to a boil in a large pot. Add pasta. Return to rapid boil. Lower heat and cook, uncovered, for 12 minutes.

7. While pasta is cooking, mix all the dressing ingredients in a screw-top jar.

8. Screw on top of jar and shake for 30 seconds. Set aside.

9. Drain pasta in a colander. Rinse pasta in cold water. Transfer to a large bowl.

10. Add everything (broccoli, peppers, dressing, basil, parsley, garlic, and Parmesan) to the pasta. Mix and chill. Serve cold.

The Boy Who Discovered the Spring

BY RAYMOND MACDONALD ALDEN
ADAPTED BY SHERI BROWNRIGG

There came once a little boy named Anza to live on this earth. He was so much pleased with it that he stayed, never caring to go back to his own world. I do not know where his own world was, or just how he came to leave it. Some thought that he was dropped by accident from some falling star. But no one knew for certain, as he never told anyone; and it did not matter, since he liked the earth so much that he did not care to leave it.

There was a man named Hoehn who lived in the valley where the little boy had first come. He had a room in his house for a visitor, and he took Anza in. They grew to like each other so well that again the little boy did not care to go away, nor did Hoehn care to have him leave. Hoehn had not always lived alone, but he had become a sorrowful man. The reason was that his only child had died. It seemed to Hoehn that there was nothing worth living for after that happened. So he moved to the lonely valley, and I suppose would have spent the rest of his life by himself, if it had not been for Anza.

It was a very lovely valley, with great green meadows that sloped down to a rippling brook. In summertime it was full of red and white and yellow blossoms. Over the brook there hung green trees, whose roots made pleasant places to rest when one was tired; and along the water's edge there grew blue flowers, while many little frogs and other live creatures played there. It was summertime when Anza came, and the flowers and the trees and the brook and the frogs made him very happy. I think that in the world from which he came they did not have such things; it was made chiefly of gold and silver and precious stones, instead of things that grow and blossom and keep one company. Anza did not ask to go to play in the town over the hills, but was quite happy with the meadows and the brookside. The only thing that did not please him was that Hoehn was still sad, thinking always of his child who had died. Anza did not understand this, for in the world from which he came nothing ever died, and he thought it strange that if Hoehn's child had died he did not patiently wait for him to come back again.

The summer went merrily on. Anza learned the names of all the flowers in the meadow and loved them dearly. He also became friends with the birds. They would come to him for crumbs, and sit on the branches close by to sing to him. The frogs would do the

same thing, and although Anza did not think their voices as sweet as those of the birds, he was too polite to let them know it.

But when September came, there began to be changes to the beautiful valley. The first thing Anza noticed was that the birds began to disappear from the meadows. Hoehn told him they had gone to make their visit to the Southland, and would come back again. At first Anza believed this. But as time went on, and the air became more and more still as the last of the birds took flight, Anza began to believe they would never come again.

At the same time the flowers began to disappear from the meadows. Anza thought, "this is what the word 'dead' means." At first others came to take their places. He tried to like the flowers of autumn as well as those which he had known first. But as these faded and dropped off, none came after them. The mornings grew colder, and the leaves on the trees were changing. They grew red and yellow, instead of green. This was interesting for Anza. But when the leaves began to fall, he was very sad. One day, every limb was bare, except for a few dried leaves at the top of one of the tallest trees. Anza grew even sadder.

One morning he went out early to see what dreadful thing might have happened in the night, for it seemed now that every night took something beautiful out of the world. He made his way toward the brook, but when he reached the place where he usually heard it, he could not hear a sound. Everything was still. Then he ran as fast as he could to the side of the brook. Sure enough, it had stopped running. Not only that, but it was covered with a hard sheet of ice.

Anza turned and ran back to Hoehn's house. Tears were running down his cheeks.

"Why, what is the matter?" asked Hoehn.

"The brook is dead," said Anza.

"I think not," said Hoehn. "It is frozen over, but it will sing to you again."

"No," said Anza. "You told me that the birds would come back, and they have not come. You told me that the trees were not dead, but every one of their leaves has gone. You told me that the flowers had seeds that did not die, and would make other flowers. I cannot find them. The meadow is bare and dark. Even the grass is not green any more. It is a dead world. Dead! Now I do not see how anyone in this world can be happy."

Hoehn thought it would be of no use to try to explain any more to Anza. He said, "Be patient," and tried to find some things for Anza to do inside the house to make him forget the outside world.

The next time they went for a walk to the town over the hill, Anza was very curious to see whether the same thing had happened there that had happened in their valley. Of course it had: the trees there seemed dead, too, and the flowers were all gone from the yards. Anza expected that everyone in the town would now be as sad as Hoehn and himself. But he was very much surprised when he saw them looking as cheerful as ever. There were some boys playing on the street corner who seemed to be as happy as boys could be. Anza asked one of them, "How can you play, when such a dreadful thing has happened to the world?"

"Why, what has happened?"

"The flowers and trees are dead," said Anza, "and the birds are gone. The brook is frozen, and the meadow is bare and gray. And it is so on this side of the hill also."

Then the boys in the street thought Anza was making a joke and they laughed. As they went on through the town, Anza wondered how the people could still be so happy.

As winter came, Hoehn found many things for Anza to do in the house. Anza grew interested in them and was not always sad. But still, if it were not that he had become very fond of Hoehn, he would have wished to go back to the world from which he had come. Hoehn would miss him too much if he should go away. He thought that they must be the only two people who really understood how sad a place the earth is.

Weeks went by. One day in March, as Anza and Hoehn were reading, they heard drops of water falling from the roof. The snow was melting from the sunshine.

"Do you want to take a little walk down toward the brook?" asked Hoehn. "I should not wonder if I could prove to you today that it has not forgotten how to talk to you."

"Yes," said Anza, though he did not think Hoehn could be right. It was months since he had cared to visit the brook.

When they reached the foot of the hillside the sheet of ice was still there.

"Put your ear down on the ice and listen," Hoehn said.

As Anza did this, he heard, as plainly as though there were no ice between, the voice of the brook gurgling in the bottom of its bed. He clapped his hands for joy.

"It is waking up, you see," said Hoehn. "Other things will wake up, too."

Anza did not know what to think, but he waited day after day with his eyes and ears wide open to see if anything else might happen. And wonderful things did happen. The

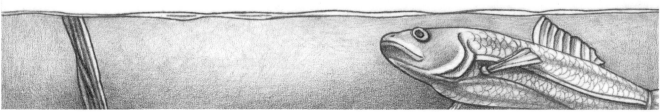

brook sang more and more, and at last broke through its cold ice coverlet and went danc-ing. One morning, while the snow was still around the house, Anza heard a chirping sound, and, looking from his window, saw a red robin.

"Have you really come back again?"

"Certainly," said the robin, "don't you know it is almost spring?"

But Anza did not understand what he said.

There was a pussy willow growing by the brook, and Anza's next discovery was that hundreds of little gray buds were coming out. He watched them grow bigger from day to day, and while he was doing this the snow was melting away in great patches where the sun shone warmest on the meadow, and the blades of grass that came up into the daylight were greener than anything Anza had ever seen.

Then the pink buds came on the maple trees, and unfolded day by day. And the fruit trees in Hoehn's orchard were as white with blossoms as they had lately been with snow.

"Not a single tree is dead," said Anza.

Last of all came the wildflowers—blue and white violets near the brook, dandelions around the house, and, a little later, yellow buttercups all over the meadow. Slowly but steadily the world was made over, until it glowed with white and green and gold. "This is even more beautiful than it was in the summertime!" Anza said.

He was wild with joy. One by one his old nature friends came back. He could not bear to stay in the house for many minutes from morning to night. Now he knew what wise Hoehn had meant by saying, "Be patient," and he began to wonder again now Hoehn could still be sorrowful in such a beautiful world.

One morning the church bells in the town rang much longer and more joyfully than usual. Anza asked Hoehn what was happening. Hoehn looked at his calendar, and answered, "Why, it is Easter. The town people celebrate it on one Sunday every spring."

"May we see?" asked Anza. It was the first time he had ever asked to go to town, so Hoehn did not say no.

The town was glowing with flowers. There were many fruit trees, and they, too, were in blossom. Almost everyone who passed along the street was wearing pretty hats. Along the sidewalks were pots of white Easter lilies. This was a beautiful sight. Suddenly there came a burst of music from where the crowd was. To Anza it seemed like the most beautiful sound he had ever heard. They did not have music in the world where he had come from. He put his fin-ger on his lips to show Hoehn that he wanted to listen. These were the words they sang:

"Spring is here, it looks like spring is here. That which was dead is alive again. That which was gone has returned! Happy Easter, spring is here."

"I do not believe that anything ever really dies," Anza said.

Hoehn looked down at him and smiled. "Perhaps not," he said. They moved in closer to the crowd. Hoehn picked up Anza and put him on his shoulders.

The music began again. And much to Anza's surprise, Hoehn sang the Easter song with the others and taught Anza the words, too. It was the first time Hoehn had sung in many years, and the first time Anza had ever sung at all. But for both of them, this was cer-tainly not the last.

Butterfly Card

Here is a spring greeting card to make for a friend. This card reminds us of caterpillars changing into butterflies. When the outside of this card is folded completely back, then moved up and down, the butterfly inside will fly.

MATERIALS

1 7 x 11-inch piece of yellow posterboard

12-inch ruler

X-Acto knife

Black marker

White glue

16 ½-inch black pompoms

Hole punch

1 6½ x 10½-inch piece of white card stock

Brightly colored markers

Glitter (optional)

1 12-inch black pipe cleaner

1 8 x 10-inch envelope

STEPS

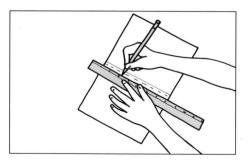

1. *Measure and score:* Place yellow posterboard on table with the long side facing you. Find center of posterboard (5½ inches from the short side) by using ruler. Make a light mark with a pencil. Measure ½ inch on either side of the center mark and make another mark. Turn the board around and mark the same places on the opposite side. Draw lines up and down the board at the ½-inch marks. Have an adult use the ruler and X-Acto knife to lightly score the lines. (**Do not cut all the way through the card.**) The scored side is the outside of the card.

2. *Write:* On the right side of the outside of card, at the top, write a spring message in black. Come up with your own or use this one: "Know how to tell when it's spring?"

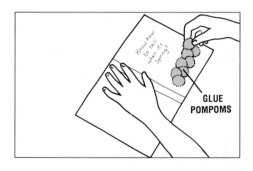

3. *Glue:* Just below the message, glue 8 pompoms touching each other in a wiggly line to make a caterpillar.

4. *Punch and glue:* Make caterpillar eyes by punching 2 holes from the edge of the white card stock. Add a dot of black to each white circle with the marker. Glue eyes on the last pompom to the right.

5. *Draw:* With black marker, draw short straight lines for legs below bottom 3 pompoms.

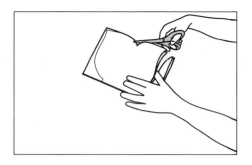

6. *Fold and draw:* Fold the white card stock in half, so it is 6½ x 5¼ inches. The fold is the center of the butterfly body. Draw butterfly wings from the folded center (as shown). The shape is similar to a number 3, but the top curve is much bigger than the bottom and the corners are pointed. With the paper folded, cut along the wings. **Do not cut on the fold.** The inside is the right side.

7. *Decorate:* Color both sides of the butterfly with colored markers. You can make your butterfly look real or make-believe. If you want to add glitter, apply a small amount of glue where you would like the glitter to go. Sprinkle glitter over the glue spots and let dry. Shake off loose glitter.

8. *Glue:* Glue 8 pompoms in a straight line down the center of the butterfly body. Let dry.

Easter

The air is like a butterfly
With frail blue wings,
The happy earth looks at the sky
And sings.

— Joyce Kilmer

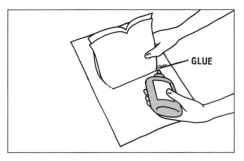

9. *Turn and glue:* Turn yellow card inside out. (Caterpillar is turned face down.) Glue center of wrong side of butterfly to center section of inside of yellow card. Be careful not to glue the wings. Let the card dry about 10 minutes.

10. *Fold and glue:* Fold pipe cleaner in half and glue at the butterfly's head as antennae. Let dry about 10 minutes.

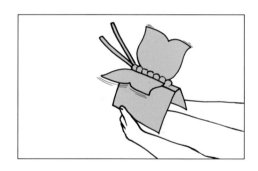

11. *Fly:* When butterfly is dry, test its flying ability by folding the card completely open onto itself. (Caterpillar is on inside.) Move yellow card up and down. Butterfly wings should flap.

12. *Envelope:* Slip your butterfly card in the envelope and address it to the lucky person who is to receive this beautiful creation.

CHAPTER TWO

Parades
and Bonnets

Easter is an entire season made up of many special days. And all of the special days, like Ash Wednesday, Good Friday, and Easter Sunday itself, are celebrated in ways that recall Christ's last days on earth. There is even a special way to get ready for the Easter season: a big parade and party in New Orleans called Mardi Gras (MAR-dee grah).

Mardi Gras is French for "Fat Tuesday," the Tuesday before Ash Wednesday, the day that marks the beginning of the forty days of Lenten fasting. On the church calendar this day is called Shrove Tuesday.

Meats, eggs, and fats were once strictly forbidden to Christians during Lent; these rules were made to help us remember Jesus' forty-day fast in the desert. So everyone made sure they ate their fill before the fast started. What better way to celebrate than by having a big parade? Now, though many people are not as strict about the fasting, they still have the big parade on "Fat Tuesday."

Children have extra fun, too, just before the serious season of Lent. Maybe they stay up a little later at night or play more practical jokes than usual. The week of Mardi Gras is a time for parades, music, carnivals, and craziness.

The famous Mardi Gras celebration was started in New Orleans over two hundred years ago by French people who came to live in Louisiana. Today it is a spectacular carnival, with thousands of masked and costumed people dancing through the streets behind bands and floats of great splendor. And riding upon the floats, as if in a fairy-tale landscape, are the king and queen of Mardi Gras and their royal court.

But the music and dancing must stop at the stroke of midnight, when Ash Wednesday arrives. For forty days the Christians of the world wait in quiet and reflection. Then, on

Grandma's Easter Bonnet

Grandma's bonnet flutters to her head
   each April

to be pinned in place by translucent
   fingers.

It has been sleeping, silently sleeping in
   a round cardboard nest,

sleeping, sleeping in the darkest corner
   of her closet,

Like a robin that reappears each spring,
   it returns to its proper perch,

quietly preening in the soft sunshine,
   ready for Easter Sunday.

— Bobbi Katz

The Easter Parade

What shall I wear for the Easter
Parade?

A dress that's the color of marmalade

With a border embroidered in light
blue cornflowers

Like the edge of a meadow after spring
showers

And a matching hat round as a top you
can spin

And elastic to hold it on under my chin

And brand-new shoes whiter than newly
poured cream

With heart-shaped, golden buckles that
gleam;

And I'll carry a small purse of butterfly
blue

With a penny for me and a penny for
you

To buy us both glasses of cold
lemonade

When we walk, hand in hand, in the
Easter Parade.

— William Jay Smith

Easter Sunday, they are joyful as they remember that Jesus came back to life and brought a new beginning.

People also have serious and solemn Easter parades. During Holy Week in towns and villages of Spain and Mexico, sacred statues are carried through the streets. In Italy on Good Friday, choirboys parade with tall, lit candles behind a replica of the coffin of Christ.

As the sun peeks up over the earth's horizon on Easter Sunday, some people get up early to attend a church service held outdoors as the sun rises. Later, other services are held in churches. All the churches, small country chapels, and large city cathedrals ring with the beautiful Easter hymns.

The tradition of wearing new clothes on Easter Sunday began when early Christians who were baptized during the Easter service wore new white robes. Also, new Easter attire has been associated with the concept of a fresh beginning. Some women and children wear Easter bonnets, hats specially decorated with flowers and other ornaments.

When the church services are over, people stroll down the avenues or in the parks, for it is a very joyous day. New York City has a wonderful parade on Fifth Avenue, in which some fifty thousand people wish each other "Happy Easter." There are no floats or bands—just people.

One of the oldest Easter parades in the United States started in Atlantic City, New Jersey, in 1876. Today, prizes are awarded there for the most unusual bonnets. Another parade, the Parada de los Caballos y Coshes (pa-RA-da day los ka-BA-yos ee KO-shes) is held in St. Augustine, Florida. In this parade there are horse-drawn Spanish carriages, decorated floats, drill teams, beauty queens, and people dressed in Spanish armor and costumes. The most famous feature of the St. Augustine Easter parade is the elaborate headgear worn by the carriage horses. These could be the best Easter bonnets ever.

The Easter Season, a time of reflection, renewal, and joyous celebration, begins and ends with great parades. Whether dancing in the Mardi Gras parade or walking in New York's Fifth Avenue parade, you'll want to be wearing an Easter bonnet.

Maybe the most well-known carnival is in Rio de Janeiro (REE-o day zha-NAIR-o), the capital of Brazil. The Brazilians set the standards for floats and costumes now copied all over the world. There is a contest each year for selecting the songs that will be played at the carnival.

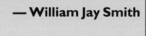

During the celebration of Carnival in Rio de Janeiro, which lasts for several days, one day all the activities are just for children. The best event is the children's parade, when boys and girls get to walk through the streets in their fancy costumes.

Party Smoothies

A smoothie is a thick drink made in a blender. It can have crushed ice, yogurt, or some-times bananas in it. This smoothie is different from any other, not because of what's inside it, but because of what's on top. This smoothie's top pops!

INGREDIENTS FOR 5 1-CUP SMOOTHIES

2 mangoes

2 oranges

1 tablespoon sugar

2 cups water

1 cup plain yogurt

2 packages (0.65 oz each) sour lemon crackling candy (use Crazy Dips, Pop Rocks, or similar candy that pops when it gets wet)

1. Peel and seed mangoes and oranges (do not remove the membrane of the oranges).

2. Mix all ingredients except the crackling candy in a blender on medium speed until smooth.

3. Pour into glasses.

4. Just before handing this to your party guest, sprinkle about ½ teaspoon crackling candy on top.

Variation: Paradesicles

1. Make smoothies as described above, but leave off the crackling candy.

2. Pour mixture into paper cups and place in freezer for 30 minutes. Remove from freezer and stick small plastic forks or wooden popsicle sticks in each cup. Return to freezer for at least 3 more hours.

3. Tear off paper cups before eating.

Secrets at the Mardi Gras

BY JOAN AND JOSEPHINE COSTANTINO
ADAPTED BY SHERI BROWNRIGG

"Tomorrow is the day!" said Victor to his friend Emile. It was the day before Mardi Gras.

Mardi Gras is a big party that is held in the streets of New Orleans. Masqueraders dance in the public squares. Prancing horses and glittering floats parade through the town. There is even a mysterious king who rides on the most magnificent float of all.

As they did every year, Victor and Emile wondered what the floats would be like. Very few people knew that the floats were built in great empty warehouses along the river. The only people who ever saw the floats before the parade were the people who made them.

Victor's father was one of the lucky few who worked on the floats. He had helped to make them for many years. All of Victor's friends were envious because Victor got to take his father's dinner to him at the warehouse. Of course Victor could not go inside. But he could go right up to the big front door where Old Jacques sat keeping guard.

Tonight was the last night Victor would visit the warehouse. Tomorrow, the work on the floats would be revealed. Victor and Emile started off with dinner for Victor's father.

"What's the big float going to be like this year, Victor?"

"I don't know. It's a surprise."

"You ought to know," said Emile. "Hasn't your father told you?"

"Of course not," said Victor. "My father would never tell."

"I dare you to find out what the big float looks like," said Emile.

"Nobody is allowed in the warehouse," said Victor. "I told you!"

"I double-dare you," said Emile. "Are you afraid?"

"No," Victor said. "Nobody is supposed to see the floats until the parade."

"If you get inside the warehouse, I'll buy you a snowcone," said Emile. "I have the money right here. You know how good they are."

Victor thought about the cold, sweet taste of a snowcone, a big cup of ice with specially flavored syrup poured over it.

"Bring me proof you have been in the warehouse, Victor. When I see the proof I will buy you a snowcone. What do you say?"

Victor didn't say anything.

"Okay, two, I'll give you two snowcones!"

"All right, Emile," he said. "I will bring you a decoration from the big float."

Victor knew it was going to be hard to get into the closely guarded warehouse. The windows in the building were high up and the side doors were kept locked. Perhaps he could get in with the help of his friend, the guard.

Old Jacques sat on a keg in front of the door, keeping watch.

"Hello, Jacques," said Victor.

"*Bon soir*," said Jacques, who spoke French as well as English.

"They are working hard in there to finish the floats by tomorrow," said Jacques. Every person has been working hard since last spring and now it is February. But it is worth all the hard work, you will see. The big float is a beauty!"

"Emile and I were wondering," Victor said, "Is there any way we could see it?"

"What?" cried Jacques. "What are you saying?"

"If you would just let me in for a peek," said Victor.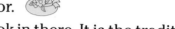

"Ha!" cried Jacques. "You know I can't let you look in there. It is the tradition of Mardi Gras that no one except the workers see the floats until the parade."

With that, Jacques took the dinner in to Victor's father, but Victor and Emile hid around the corner from Jacques' post and sat down to think. Maybe they could prop open the door while Jacques wasn't looking. Soon, Old Jacques came back outside and began to move the barrels from the yard into the building.

The boys looked at each other. "This is your chance," said Emile.

Victor knew what his friend meant. While Jacques was inside, he ran to another barrel and jumped inside. Before he pulled down the lid, he said, "Run away before Jacques comes back and sees you."

"Good luck," Emile whispered and hurried off.

The barrel was quite small. There was not much room to stretch. Victor was afraid if he took a deep breath he would split the sides of the barrel. How dark it was! And how still!

After a while he heard Jacques come back. Then he felt the barrel moving. Up! Up!

Jacques groaned. "Goodness, these barrels are getting heavier as I get older."

Victor heard the sound of Jacques' footsteps on a wooden floor. Then he felt the barrel being lowered. Down! Down! He heard Jacques' footsteps going away. He heard the sound of men's voices and the creaking of saws and the tap-tap of hammers. There was a tiny knothole in the barrel and Victor put one eye to the small opening. All he could see was Jacques' legs moving up the steps and the legs of the workmen in the shadows.

It was so warm inside the barrel that Victor began to feel sleepy. Soon he fell asleep. When he woke up there was not a sound to be heard anywhere. The hammers had stopped.

Victor pushed up the lid. All the men had gone home. He was alone in the building. His legs were stiff and cramped but he managed to climb out of the barrel.

Silvery moonlight shone through the high windows onto something big and shiny in the middle of the room, something that sparkled in the moonlight.

Victor walked closer. It was a float! The big float. It looked like a giant wedding cake covered with tinsel and flowers. There was a throne in the center of the float. This had to be the float that Rex, the King of the Carnival, would ride in tomorrow.

Victor was almost afraid to reach out his hand and touch the shining carriage for fear it would dissolve into moonlight. He walked round and round the float, feasting his eyes on it. How wonderful it was! Then he remembered that he must bring Emile something to prove that he had really seen it.

There was a pretty border of silver leaves around the edge of the float. Victor was very careful not to spoil the border. He chose a tiny silver leaf from the back where it wouldn't be missed. Victor put the leaf into his pocket and then, with a last look at the dazzling float, ran up the stairs and out the door into the night.

When he got home, Victor went straight to bed to make sure he got enough sleep for his big day tomorrow. He hid the silver leaf under his pillow to keep it safe until morning.

Victor woke up with a start when he heard the ping of pebbles hitting his window. He looked out. A green goblin wearing a mask jumped and somersaulted gaily.

"Hurry up, hurry up," the green goblin called.

Victor recognized Emile's voice and called back, "C'mon in! I'll be right down."

Victor's mother helped him put on the bright purple goblin suit she had made for him. Green, yellow, and purple are the three colors of Mardi Gras.

When Victor's father saw the goblins he said, "I'll bet you two will be right up front to watch the parade. Just wait until you see the big float!"

"I've already seen it," Victor whispered to Emile. "Look, I brought you a silver leaf from it."

"When you show me the place where the silver leaf came from, I will buy you the snowcones," Emile promised.

The two goblins dashed off, darting in and out of the crowds, stopping to stare at pretty girls selling flowers and peddlers offering cotton candy, bright clouds of balloons, and bags of peanuts and popcorn. Bells tinkled. Horns blew. Everyone in the street wore a mask. There were masks that looked like heads of animals. There were clowns and grinning skulls and devils with horns, gypsies, pirates, knights, and lovely ladies. Victor and Emile felt as if they were in a dream instead of in the city of New Orleans.

At last a loud cheer rose from the crowd. "Here it comes! Here comes the parade!" Mounted policemen cleared the way for the royal attendants of King Rex. They came riding in splendor on spirited horses. They carried swords like shining tongues of flame and they were dressed in purple and gold.

The boys squeezed through the crowd and found a place right in front.

A shining mass of color and dancing light appeared in the distance. It was the beautiful float that Victor had seen the night before in the warehouse. High on the golden throne sat King Rex, smiling and nodding behind his mask.

The float was so high it almost reached the overhanging balconies that lined the street. It glittered with jewels and silver. Victor pointed to the border of silver leaves that matched the silver leaf he held in his hand.

"You see, Emile," Victor said. "I really did see the float last night."

"Yes, you did," Emile replied, his voice filled with awe.

Victor turned and looked at his friend. Emile's eyes were wide with amazement as he gazed upon the magnificent float sparkling in the sunlight. Victor almost wished he hadn't peeked and was also seeing the float for the first time.

Following the big float were dozens of other floats, swaying under the weight of flowers and ornaments and laughing masqueraders. When the parade had passed, everyone crowded into the street again and there was music and dancing and singing.

The two goblins went in search of the snowcone man. They found him pushing his little cart through the crowds. The cart was so pretty that it looked like it was part of the parade. Emile ordered, "One grape and one lime please."

Victor wondered which one to taste first. He looked at Emile . . . and back at the snowcones. Then he handed Emile the lime snowcone. "It matches your goblin costume."

The boys were silent until the last sweet, cold drop was gone.

The lights on Canal Street twinkled as they went home. They felt the cool river breeze on their flushed cheeks. Their feet were very tired. They had walked miles and miles that day.

Ah, how wonderful Mardi Gras was! They went to bed to dream of the parades they had seen, the processions of floats and masqueraders, and the color and the grandness of Mardi Gras. And how wonderful it had been to share snowcones on such a day.

Your Own Easter Bonnet

Easter is the time of the year to wear a bonnet. Pick which parade you would like to be in and make your own bonnet to wear. Use the basic instructions here for the bonnet, but come up with your own decorations to make it personal and unique.

MATERIALS

1 12 x 12-inch piece foam craft

Pen

Yarn needle

5 yards colored paper cords, wrapping wire, telephone wire, or ribbon with wire in it

12 or more ¼-inch beads

Feathers and glitter

STEPS

1. *Find center:* Find the center of one side of the foam piece by folding it in half and marking the fold lightly with a pen. Measure ½ inch from center mark in each direction and mark again.

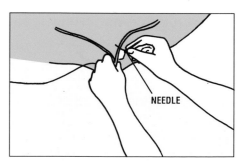

2. *Fold and tuck:* Bring the two outside marks together, folding the center up. Make a "tuck" outwards by stitching through the two thicknesses using the needle and a 3-inch piece of wire. Tie beads to the end of the wire.

3. *Repeat:* Repeat this on each of the remaining sides of the foam.

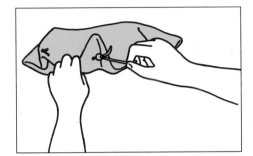

4. *Fold and tuck:* On 2 corners of the square, fold corners up to make a triangle that is at least 4 inches along the fold. On the folded edge of the triangle, measure 2 inches from center in each direction, and make a tuck like you did in the above steps. (This time you are sewing through 4 layers.)

5. *Tuck and fold:* On the other 2 corners, you will need to try the hat on to see how big these tucks need to be. Test this by pinching foam into the necessary size of tucks until the hat fits your head comfortably. Fold corners up and tuck as in step 4.

6. *Decorate:* Now is the fun part. With needle and some wire, sew on feathers and more beads. Make stitches with colored wire and leave ends long and curly.

On the island of Saint Thomas in the Virgin Islands, at the end of April, there is a week of festivities celebrating spring. A little boy and girl get to be prince and princess and march at the head of a children's parade. Babies, donkeys, and pets also join in and wear hats decorated with tassels and feathers.

CHAPTER THREE

Here Comes the Easter Bunny!

Who has long, soft ears and hops quickly out of sight, but leaves behind beautiful eggs and Easter baskets? The Easter Bunny!

Rabbits have been a part of spring festivals for a long time. For the ancient Egyptians, the rabbit was a symbol of birth because female rabbits have lots of babies. That is why they represent new life.

The hare, a close relative of the rabbit, was believed by some people in ancient Europe to have been the escort to the goddess Eostre (es-TRAY). In spring, celebrations were held in her honor. The hare was also the symbol of the Greek goddess of love. Others say that the hare (and later, the rabbit) became a part of Easter because in Egyptian mythology, it symbolized the moon, and the moon's position sets the date for Easter.

The moon has a lot to do with Easter. In the year 325, a church council met and decided that Easter would fall on the first Sunday after the first full moon following the twenty-first day of March. Since then the exact day of Easter has varied from year to year according to when the moon is full.

In old England people tried to catch rabbits on Easter. Whoever brought a rabbit to the church before ten o'clock in the morning would receive a hundred eggs for breakfast.

Have you ever wondered how we came to believe that the Easter Bunny delivers eggs on Easter? A folk tale from Bavaria tells of a poor mother who had nothing to give her children as Easter gifts. While feeding her chickens one day, she got the idea to make dyes and decorate eggs for her children. She hid a basket of the decorated eggs under a tree near the church where her children had gone for services. When the children left the church, they saw a rabbit. Following the rabbit, they

Patience

Chocolate Easter bunny
in a jelly bean nest,
I'm saving you for very last
Because I love you best.
I'll only take a nibble
From the tip of your ear
And one bite from the other side
So that you won't look queer.
Yum, you're so delicious!
I didn't meant to eat
Your chocolate tail till Tuesday.
Oops! There go your feet!
I wonder how your back tastes
With all that chocolate hair.
I never thought your tummy
Was only filled with air!
Chocolate Easter bunny
In a jelly bean nest,
I'm saving you for very last
Because I love you best.

— **Bobbi Katz**

The Easter Bunny

There's a story quite funny,

About a toy bunny,

And the wonderful things she can do;

Every bright Easter morning,

Without any warning,

She colors eggs, red, green, or blue.

Some she covers with spots,

Some with quaint little dots,

And some with strange mixed colors, too—

Red and green, blue and yellow.

But each unlike his fellow

Are the eggs of every hue.

And it's odd, as folk say,

That on no other day

In all of the whole year through,

Does this wonderful bunny,

So busy and funny,

Color eggs of every hue.

If this story you doubt

She will soon find you out,

And what do you think she will do?

On the next Easter morning

She'll bring you without warning

Those eggs of every hue!

— M. Josephine Todd

came upon the eggs, and thought the rabbit had left them as his gift. These eggs must have been so pretty that the children decided to join the fun and in the years that followed, they colored some eggs themselves. Obviously, many children have joined in the fun since then.

In Fredricksburg, Texas, about a hundred fifty years ago, some children were frightened by the flames of Indian campfires they saw on the hillsides all around the town on Easter Eve. Their parents told them not to worry. It was just the Easter Rabbit heating big kettles of dye. He was coloring eggs that he would bring to their houses during the night and leave for the children to find on Easter morning. Today the people of Fredricksburg rekindle the Easter fires annually and retell the story of the big kettles of dye.

The Easter Bunny of Germany is called Osterhafe (ester-HAHF) or "Easter hare." He is a large, quick rabbit with extra long legs and ears. Osterhafe is careful where he leaves his eggs. He likes to leave them in soft nests of leaves or hay. Most of our traditions of the Easter Bunny come from Osterhafe.

Children everywhere love the Easter Bunny. And so they should. He is so cute with his pink, twitching nose and floppy, oversized ears. If a boy or girl is quick enough, he or she may also feel how wonderfully soft a rabbit's coat is. Just one touch to the fur not only feels good, but brings good luck, too.

The Bunny Hop dance is fun to do at parties:

1. To begin, have everyone line up one behind the other and hold on to the person in front at the waist, feet together.

2. Everyone puts their right foot out to the side, then back in place again. Do this again.

3. Repeat step 2 with the left foot.

4. Everyone jumps forward once, then jumps back once.

5. Jump forward three hops.

6. Repeat steps 1 through 5.

Ginger-bread Bunnies

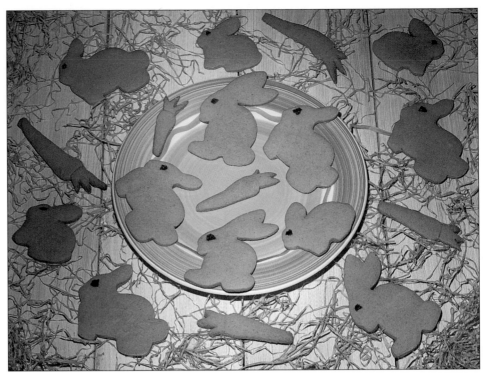

For this recipe, you will need a cookie cutter.

4 cups flour

1 teaspoon baking soda

1 teaspoon ground ginger

1 teaspoon ground cinnamon

½ teaspoon ground cloves

1 cup butter (softened)

⅔ cup brown sugar

½ cup honey

1 egg

1 teaspoon vanilla extract

Raisins

Variation:

If you do not have a bunny-shaped cookie cutter, you can easily change a bear or gingerbread man shape into a bunny by lightly laying the cutter down on the dough, and with a knife, cutting around the outline of the cutter, stopping at the head to add rabbit ears.

1. Sift flour, baking soda, ginger, cinnamon, and cloves together.

2. With a mixer, cream butter and sugar together.

3. Add honey, egg, and vanilla extract to butter-and-sugar mixture and beat for 2 minutes.

4. Add dry ingredients to mixture a little at a time and beat with mixer until well blended.

5. Make dough into a ball shape and wrap in tea towel or waxed paper. Chill in refrigerator for 30 minutes.

6. Preheat oven to 350°F.

7. Roll out dough with rolling pin on a lightly floured surface to about ¼ inch thick. To do this, it is best to place rolling pin in the center of the dough and roll out to the edge.

Repeat this in all directions to get an even thickness. Dust the dough with a little bit of flour if rolling pin sticks.

8. Dip cookie cutter in flour, place on dough, and cut out bunnies. You can also make carrot-shaped cookies for the gingerbread bunnies to eat. One way to do this is to lay a clean, dry carrot with green attached on the dough and cut around it.

9. Lightly press on raisins for eyes.

10. Place cookies on lightly greased cookie sheets and bake for approximately 8 minutes. Cool on racks.

The Rabbits

Here's a verse about rabbits
That doesn't mention their habit.

— Ogden Nash

Alice in Easterland

BY SHERI BROWNRIGG AND MARY ROBINSON
BASED ON *ALICE IN WONDERLAND*, BY LEWIS CARROLL

"Alice, would you like some more raspberry Jell-O?" asked Alice's mother. "No," Alice said. "We have Jell-O all the time. Why can't I have an Easter tart?" "Alice, you know those are for tomorrow," her mother said.

"Easter Eve dinner should be made up of Easter tarts, jelly beans, marshmallow chicks, and chocolate rabbits, and it should all be served by a beautiful white rabbit."

"Maybe when you're a mother, you can make an Easter Eve dinner just like that," her mother said. "But right now it's time for you to get a good night's sleep."

Alice was halfway up the stairs when the phone rang. It was Aunt Rose.

"They always talk forever," thought Alice. "And while they talk I can check on the Easter tarts once more."

Alice slipped into the kitchen. A dozen Easter tarts were on the counter. "They smell so good." Alice leaned closer and closer until her nose bumped a tart. A morsel of crust broke off. "Oops," Alice thought. "But it *was* an accident."

Alice walked to the kitchen door and opened it a crack. Her mother was laughing, "Aunt Rose must be telling her a good story," she thought. Alice turned back to the tarts. "Now that I've accidentally broken off a piece of that tart, maybe I should just eat it. Let's see if I can rearrange the rest so it won't look like one's missing."

She tried but couldn't; it always looked like eleven instead of twelve. And worse, before she knew it, she'd taken a bite of the one she had bumped. It tasted even better than she'd imagined. She took another bite and then another until she'd eaten the whole tart.

"Oh, no," she cried. "Wait until mother finds out."

She ran to her room and sat in the window seat, where she always sat when she felt badly. "I hope mother stays on the phone forever."

Alice's mother wasn't on the phone forever, but she was on so long that Alice started to yawn. Her tummy felt full from the tart. The last thing she thought about before she lay down on the window seat was, "I wish a white rabbit would bring my Easter goodies."

"We're late, we're late," said someone just outside her window.

"Who? What? Why, you're the White Rabbit!" exclaimed Alice.

"Hurry up, we're late," he said.

Alice threw open the window and ran after the rabbit. He popped down a large rabbit hole. Alice dove in after him.

The rabbit hole went straight down for a long way and then curved and swerved. Alice felt herself falling down and down and down. Her body moved so slowly she felt as if she were floating on a cloud. She tried to see what was ahead, but it was too dark. But she could see to the sides of the hole where there were lighted rooms. In the rooms she noticed all kinds of interesting activities. In one room Alice heard "cheep, cheep, cheep." There were thousands of little yellow fluffy baby chicks. "Chicks don't live in rabbit holes, do they?" she exclaimed. In the next room she saw paints and dyes and brushes and eggs. Suddenly, hundreds of flamingoes rushed in and began to paint the eggs. Easter eggs! "I've never seen such beautiful eggs," Alice thought. She dearly wished she could have one of the eggs.

She sniffed something and sniffed again. "Oh, what a wonderful smell."

"Hot-cross buns," a lizard yelled. "It's hot-cross buns." There were also pretzels, cakes, and cookies. "This is all very nice," said Alice, "but where are the tarts?"

Next she saw hat trimmings everywhere: lace, flowers, hat pins, ribbons. And before she could say "White Rabbit," the trimmings combined to form extraordinary Easter bonnets. Some bonnets were for boys, others for girls, and even some for rabbits.

She floated by a melted chocolate waterfall where men dressed in giant playing cards were filling metal molds to make chocolate Easter flowers. Then the chocolate flowers turned into real ones: lilies, daffodils, tulips, and crocuses.

She wanted to stop but she kept falling. Down, down, down. "I wonder if I shall fall right through the earth." She giggled.

KERPLUNK!

Suddenly Alice landed and yelled, "OUCH!" She had reached the bottom. "Why this is curious. I'm in a courtroom!" And right in front of her was the White Rabbit. "So there you are, White Rabbit. Why did you leave me?"

"Hush! I'll ask the questions," he said. "When did you last see the missing tart?"

"Just after dinner. Oh, they smelled so good," Alice said. Then she noticed the King and Queen of Hearts. "Are you the judges?" she asked them.

"Silence!" said the White Rabbit. He blew a trumpet, unrolled a parchment scroll, and read: The Queen of Hearts, she made some tarts,/Just before Easter day./We will decide if Alice stole those tarts,/and ate them all away.

"No!" Alice said. "I left the table without eating any Easter tarts."

"And after that?" White Rabbit stepped closer. His eyes narrowed. He looked at her so accusingly that Alice began to shake.

"Oh, dear. Now what?" she thought. "He's going to make me tell him I stole a tart."

Just then a silly man with a silly hat who identified himself as the Mad Hatter said, "I beg your pardon, your Majesty, but if she hasn't eaten the tarts, and she hasn't even seen the tarts since dinner, then we should all have tea."

Alice was very, very relieved. She looked around and said, "This is a funny tea party." "There's a sleeping mouse, a march hare, the White Rabbit, the Mad Hatter, and the King and Queen of Hearts. Why, everyone who is anyone is here."

"Pass the tarts," ordered the Queen of Hearts.

"There are no tarts," Alice said quietly. "And even if there were, we couldn't eat them until tomorrow."

"Pour the tea." The White Rabbit looked at his watch.

The Mad Hatter said, "Have some tea." He poured it right on top of Alice's head.

Alice felt a very curious sensation. It started in her shoulders and hips. Then it spread to her elbows and knees. Soon she felt it everywhere. "I'm growing!" Her knees hit the table. Then the chair she was sitting in broke. Her feet went flying and kicked the whole table topsy-turvier than it was to begin with. "If I don't stop, I'll turn into a giant. Help!"

"So she did eat the tarts!" exclaimed the Queen. "She would only grow if she drank the tea after she ate a tart. That test never fails. Off with her head!"

The men dressed in giant playing cards raced toward her. But Alice was growing so fast that everything around her was sucked into a wind that traveled from her feet to her nose. The playing cards were flicked up into the air and flipped over and over.

As Alice continued to grow, the wind became as strong as a giant vacuum cleaner. It sucked up everything in wider and wider circles. There was chaos everywhere.

"Oh, dear. Oh, dear," cried Alice. As she kept growing, her head traveled back up the rabbit hole. She knocked over flowers. She carved tracks in the chocolate molds with her eyelashes. And she created snarls in the Easter bonnet ribbons with her hair.

"Help! Oh, won't someone please help me!" Alice pleaded.

But she kept growing. She startled the lizard and shocked the flamingoes. And she frightened the poor little fluffy baby chicks.

POP!

Alice's head squeezed out the top of the rabbit hole and into her very own room. But her shoulders were stuck. She squirmed and shook and . . .

"Wake up, Alice dear!" said her mother, gently patting Alice's shoulder. "Did you sleep the whole night at the window? You silly girl. No wonder you're twitching."

"Oh, I've had such a curious dream." And she told her mother everything. Then she said, "I'm sorry, mother, I stole a tart."

"It was a silly, curious dream, dear. Those kinds of dreams sometimes happen when something is bothering you."

"Are you angry at me?"

"Well, dear, at first I was. But then I remembered that my mother made the best tarts in the world and I—like you—just couldn't stop myself from eating one."

"I won't ever do it again, Mother."

"I know," said her mother. "Now why don't you go see what the Easter Bunny left."

Alice raced down the stairs to the living room. And there in the middle of a big basket surrounded by colored eggs, sparkle grass, jelly beans, and marshmallow chicks, was the White Rabbit himself, pocket watch and all. Alice picked him up and went gratefully into the kitchen to her mother. The rabbit and Alice each ate two Easter tarts and drank two cups of tea. So Alice had a very nice Easter tea with the White Rabbit after all.

Kachina Rabbit

At one time the Hopi Indians believed that many little gods or spirits called *kachinas* lived among them. The Hopi make masks and dolls that represent these spirits.

Some North American Indian tribes perform a ceremonial dance called the Wa'bos (WA-boos) Dance, meaning the Rabbit Dance; their word for rabbit is <u>wa'bos</u>. During the ceremonial dance they circle a drum, crouching, pretending to put food in their mouths, and moving their lips and noses like a rabbit.

MATERIALS

- *2 2-oz. pieces natural-colored polymer clay, such as Super Sculpey ***

- *2 4-inch wood craft sticks or 2 4-inch pieces hanger wire*

- *1 2-oz. piece black polymer clay, such as Super Sculpey ***

- *Black, white, red, and blue acrylic paint, 2 oz. each*

- *1 #4 paintbrush*

- *Glass or clay baking tray or dish (do not use a metal dish)*

STEPS

1. *Knead and divide:* Knead together the two natural-colored pieces of clay until soft. Divide this into 9 equal pieces: 1 for both ears, 1 for the head, 1 for each arm, 1 for each leg, 2 for the body, and 1 for 5 eggs.

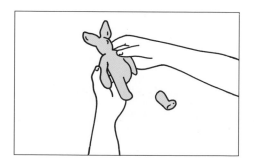

2. *Shape and connect:* Shape the different body parts as shown. Connect the parts by pushing them together, molding at the joints. You can use

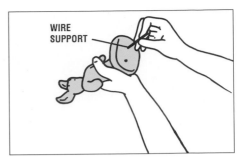

WIRE SUPPORT

the tip of a wood or wire piece to help smooth the hard-to-get-to joints.

3. *Balance:* Hold your kachina up to see if it balances. Bend your kachina where you need to. It is all right if it leans a little—the support pieces you will add will take care of this. Set your Kachina Rabbit and eggs aside while you make the base.

4. *Knead:* Unwrap the black clay. You don't need to work the black clay much because it is already close to the size you need. Just round the corners, and flatten it some by gently throwing it down on the table and pressing it with your hand. Roll it like a wheel on the table to make a round shape.

5. *Stand and support:* Stand the rabbit on the base. While holding the rabbit, have an adult help you insert the support pieces through the bottom of the base and up through the legs. You will leave these in.

6. *Bake:* Heat the oven to 275° F. Stand or lay the Kachina Rabbit and eggs in a glass or clay baking dish. Bake in oven for 15 minutes. Remove from oven and let cool for about 20 minutes.

7. *Paint:* Now you are ready to paint the Kachina Rabbit. First paint the whole body and the eggs white (leave the base black). Let dry. Paint black stripes around the figure. Add a touch of red on lips and marks on cheeks. Add dots of blue for the eyes. Paint the eggs with black and white stripes and dots of red or blue. Let dry.

*Polymer clay is available in most arts and crafts stores. Super Sculpey is one available brand; Fimo is another.

CHAPTER FOUR

Easter Baskets, Toys, and Treats

O n Easter morning it is quite likely you will be looking around the house for a special basket filled with chocolate goodies, jelly beans, cream eggs and real eggs, toys, and other treats.

This tradition may have been started by the children of mountainous Austria, who used their baskets in a slightly different way. On the Saturday before Easter they walked from farm to farm, singing and begging for eggs to fill the baskets. Everywhere the children stopped, farm women brought out beautifully decorated eggs and presented them to the singers.

Yet another way we have come to have wonderful Easter baskets dates back to olden times. On the Saturday before Easter, Russian Orthodox Christians and others of Slavic origin prepared to end their Lenten fast by taking baskets of food to their churches for the Blessing of the Pascha (PAH-sha) Baskets. These baskets were filled with foods forbidden during the Lenten season—typically bread, lamb, butter, cheese, salt, colored eggs, and other foods. After the priest blessed the baskets, the food was taken home to be eaten.

From these practices came the tradition of the Easter Bunny delivering treats in a beautiful basket. But he didn't always leave his gifts indoors, nor were they always left in a basket. In Germany and Switzerland, boys and girls made leafy nests in their yards for the Easter Bunny to fill with eggs. If you take a good look at a basket, you'll notice it is a lot like a nest.

In fact, children in many countries made nests instead of baskets—sometimes out of hay, sometimes out of grass and twigs, and sometimes even out of stones, as Irish children used to do. But these Irish children didn't wait for the Easter Bunny. They spent the week before Easter gathering all the duck and goose eggs they could find and putting them away in their stone

Questions about Easter Baskets

How does the Easter bunny get
my purple Easter basket?
That bunny works so secretly,
who has a chance to ask it?

When I've played in the attic,
I've seen baskets on a shelf.
Who brings them to the bunny?
Does it climb up there itself?

If the bunny needs some jellybeans,
there are extras at the store.
And as for eggs, it has its own,
so why would it need more?

I'm glad that it recycles,
but still I'd like to ask it,
"Easter Bunny, tell me please,
how did you get my basket?"

— **Bobbi Katz**

Easter Basket

A basket! A basket! I found a little
 basket!

I found it underneath my bed

I wonder how it got there?

It's Easter! It's Easter! I know that it is
 Easter.

Just look at all the colored eggs

And candy in my basket!

A bunny! A bunny! I know a bunny left
 it;

For who could crawl beneath my bed

Unless it was a bunny?

He likes me! He likes me! I know that
 bunny likes me;

For here's a chocolate Easter egg

And jelly beans to chew on!

I know it! I know it! I know the bunny
 left it;

For here's a note addressed to me,

It says, "Love from the Bunny!"

(Spoken at the end:) SINCE WHEN
COULD BUNNIES WRITE?

— Robert Quackenbush

hiding places. Then, on Easter Sunday, they gave the eggs to special friends and to younger children.

Children of German settlers in Pennsylvania years ago didn't use baskets or nests to gather their eggs. The boys used their caps and the girls used their bonnets. They would hide their hats around the house, hoping the Easter Bunny would fill them with eggs.

In most places around the world, the Easter Bunny leaves wonderful Easter goodies. English children are given large chocolate eggs wrapped in colorful paper. Austrian boys and girls might receive hollow imitation eggs covered with wonderful designs and holding small treasures inside.

In many parts of the world, small replicas of the Easter Bunny are made out of chocolate. These can be as small as one inch or as gigantic as three feet tall. Have you ever wondered how hollow chocolate Easter Bunnies are made? Liquid chocolate is poured into a double-sided mold that is clamped shut. The mold is then spun very fast and the chocolate inside moves into every nook and cranny of the mold. This creates the hollow space in the center of the bunny. The mold is left to cool, and the chocolate shrinks a little. The bunny frees itself from the sides of the mold and hops out.

Jelly beans are a popular Easter candy. Shaped like tiny Easter eggs, jelly beans are made of soft, molded jelly that is coated by tumbling in pans of syrup and sugar, which becomes hard when dried. Today, these treats come in almost any flavor—even popcorn, coconut, bubble gum, and peanut butter.

The Easter Bunny is everywhere at Easter, delivering eggs, toys, and treats to children. Easter is a special, fun time of the year, and well worth waiting for through the winter.

A very fun spring tradition in the United States is the giving of May baskets. On May 1, children make paper baskets and fill them with flowers. They secretly place them on the doorknobs or doorsteps of a neighbor's house. Then they ring the doorbell or knock, and before someone answers, the children run away, leaving the neighbor a delightful surprise.

In Mexico children make special toys for Holy Week. The most popular are little papier-mâché Judas dolls and wooden rattles. The Judas doll stands for the biblical character Judas, who was the person who betrayed Jesus in his last days on earth. Wooden rattles are played with to make noise.

Marzipan Chicks

Baby chicks are such a sweet part of Easter. Here is a recipe for making chick treats you can eat.

INGREDIENTS FOR 20 CHICKS

7 oz. marzipan

⅓ cup raisins

½ cup chopped walnuts

20 4-inch wooden craft sticks

1 10-oz. package white chocolate chips

1 tablespoon butter

Yellow, brown, and orange cake-decorating gel

1. Knead marzipan, raisins, and walnuts together using your hands. Shape into 20 round balls.

2. Stick a wooden craft stick ½ inch into each ball. Be careful not to break the ball or poke through the other side. Lay these on a dish and place in the freezer while you are making the coating.

3. Place white chocolate chips and butter in a microwaveable bowl or in the top of a double boiler. Heat butter-and-chocolate mixture in microwave on high for 30 seconds, then stir. If melting on the stove, melt mixture over medium heat, stirring every once in a while until mixture is creamy and smooth. When coating is melted, add a small dab, about ⅛ teaspoon, of yellow decorating gel to get the chick color.

4. Remove marzipan balls from freezer. Leave the sticks on. While holding a stick, use a small spatula or icing knife to spread the coating on the ball. This is difficult, so take your time to make these as smooth as you can.

5. When you have finished coating a marzipan ball, stick it in an upside-down paper cup in the bottom of which you have made 3 or 4 cuts. Each cup will hold about three to four balls.

6. Repeat with the other balls.

7. With the tube of yellow decorating gel, create a head directly on the body by squeezing a round ball of gel. Let set a few minutes.

8. On the head, add beak by squeezing a triangle shape of orange decorating gel. With brown decorating gel, squeeze two dots for eyes. With the yellow gel, add half-moon shapes on the side of body for wings.

9. When the icing has set, remove chicks from the sticks. You can serve on a plate or wrap each chick in plastic and tie with a ribbon.

A Tisket, A Tasket

A tisket, a tasket,

A green-and-yellow basket.

I wrote a letter to my love,

And on the way I dropped it.

I dropped it, I dropped it.

And on the way I dropped it.

A little boy (girl) picked it up,

And put it in his (her) pocket.

Abbott's Habit

BY SHERI BROWNRIGG

You may have heard of the Cravetts. The Cravetts were the first family of rabbits to paint and deliver Easter eggs to children. There was Mother Cravett, Father Cravett, six girl Cravetts, and six boy Cravetts, including Abbott.

Abbott was the youngest, too young to help much with the egg decorating. He couldn't wait until he could join his family painting Easter eggs. Each year he had tried, but each year his brothers and sisters said: "Great colors! What wonderful bold strokes! Too bad the lines aren't straight enough for our Easter eggs."

Then his parents said, "Don't worry, Abbott. You're still a bunny, honey. Keep practicing. Maybe next year."

So Abbott would practice and experiment with paint, and sometimes try to make something his family could deliver for Easter. He practiced on large rocks and small stones. Once he even painted his own face, but his brothers laughed and said, "Abbott, you look so cute. Little guy, you're always trying to make us laugh."

Another time Abbott painted a tree in the front yard, but his sisters said, "It's beautiful, Abbott, but trees can't be delivered to children, you sweet little bunny."

"Maybe I'm a little guy, maybe I'm just a little bunny. But I'm still a Cravett! I want to help with Easter," Abbott insisted, and then he went off with paints and brushes to prove that he could be of help to the family.

Abbott went off so often, that if someone asked where he was and what he was doing, his mother and father would say, "Oh, Abbott's got a habit of experimenting." Then his sisters and brothers would giggle and sing, "Abbott's got a habit, Abbott's got a habit. Cute little funny bunny."

This year, the family set up shop in the basement, just like they did every year. They formed a long assembly line of rabbits. Each one painted something wonderful and different on each egg. Everyone enjoyed their job making the eggs.

One morning, Abbott stood at the top of the stairs and heard how happy everyone was. He wanted so much to be a part of the production. When he could no longer bear listening to their singing fun, he left to go outdoors with his paints and brushes.

Abbott walked through the woods, looking for something new to practice on. Suddenly, a wonderful glistening pattern of stretched strings caught his eye.

He walked closer. "Wow, this isn't string. It's a spider web. A *real* spider web." The only spider web Abbott had ever seen was one that was part of a Halloween decoration. He stared at the web for a long time. "It would be interesting to paint this," Abbott mused. But then he saw the spider, and he remembered that the web was her home. "Hello, Spider," he said to her and decided to leave the web as he found it.

Instead, Abbott set his paints and brushes down, for he had decided to make his own spider web. He found some long blades of grass. He took six of them and arranged them on the ground so they looked like spokes on a bicycle wheel.

"How can I stick them together?" he asked the spider, who had been watching him.

"Try weaving another long blade, over and under the other spokes," she advised.

He wove a blade in a circle and discovered that if he had an uneven number of spokes, the web held together very nicely. Then, he painted it. Abbott held his creation up so Spider could see.

"Pretty good." Spider said, "I could use someone like you to help me out."

"I wish my family wanted me to help out." Abbott held his web in one of his hands. He started thinking how this had nothing to do with Easter. "This is not an Easter egg, or anything that can help in the family business."

"I still think it's very pretty, and that you should take it home to show your parents," Spider counseled. "I think they would enjoy seeing what you invented today."

So Abbott piled his paints and brushes on top of his spider web, and picked everything up by grabbing the edges of the web. Its middle curved down so that it was shaped like a bowl, with the paints carried neatly inside.

"Hey look, Spider!"

"I like that," Spider said. "You should show your family."

Abbott took his creation home, but before he could show it to his mother, she called everyone for lunch and all his brothers and sisters came running upstairs. Abbott was worried that his invention would be ruined in the crush, so he decided to put it in his room and show his mother later.

"I can't wait to hear about your morning," his mother said when he returned to the kitchen. "You won't believe what a morning we had in the basement egg factory."

One of his sisters said, "You should have been there. But I guess you were painting other things, like your hand." The children laughed.

Abbott looked at his hand. When he painted the web, he had gotten paint on himself as well.

"Now, now," said his father. "Abbott's got a nice habit of experimenting. You never know, he may paint or invent something important one of these days."

Abbott knew his father would be interested in his new creation, but he didn't want to show the web in front of his brothers and sisters. They laughed at everything he did.

After lunch, Abbott went to his room. He played with his web, which was still in the shape of a bowl. Looking in the mirror, he put it on his head for a hat. Then he trapped a bug in it to see if it would work as a cage, but the bug crawled out from between the spokes. He tried it over his light as a shade. Then he filled it with marbles. "This is my favorite way of using it, to hold things."

"Abbott, where did you get that basket?" Abbott didn't know it, but his father had been watching him from the doorway.

"Basket? Oh, this. I—I made it. Do you like it, Father?"

"I like your basket a lot, Abbott. I need a basket like that. Could you make me a big one to use in the factory?"

"You bet!" Abbott shouted.

He raced back to Spider, who was happy to hear Abbott's good news. Abbott pulled out grass by the bundles and started to work. First, he arranged spokes, then wove blades in and out, in and out. As he was nearing the end, he pulled the grass tighter, making the spokes curl up even higher.

When the web was the size he wanted, he twisted several pieces of grass into a handle. He painted the new basket with bold, fat strokes of purple and red. The basket held its shape, the handle even stayed on, and Abbott loved it.

"Wow, you are truly gifted," Spider said. "What a beautiful basket!"

"I hope my family thinks the same thing."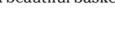

"I'm sure they will," replied Spider.

Abbott said goodbye to Spider and headed home. He entered the house with his basket behind his back, worried that his brothers and sisters were upstairs. But he found only his mother, who was having tea in the kitchen.

"What are you doing, Abbott? Is that something you made? Let me see," she said when she saw him.

He pulled the basket from behind his back and presented it to her.

"Why, Abbott, that's beautiful," she exclaimed. "You made that? Father! Father!" she yelled into the basement. "Come see what Abbott has made."

Abbott heard sounds of stomping and galloping as his father came into the kitchen. Behind him were Abbott's brothers and sisters.

"Oh, dear," worried Abbott. "What if they laugh at my basket?"

But his brothers and sisters exclaimed: "Wow! Neat! Cool!"

His father examined the basket. Then he said, "You have made something really useful, Abbott. This basket is so terrific I'll deliver Easter eggs in it."

"Yes," his mother said. "Abbott, please make some more baskets so we can deliver eggs in them. Then we won't have to just leave the eggs in the grass anymore."

"I'll set up a spot for you to make baskets in our factory," said his father. Several brothers and sisters offered to help Abbott make baskets.

Abbott sighed happily. "Now I really feel like a true Cravett."

Abbott's wish had finally come true. But each year his parents still encouraged him to go off and experiment. And when he did, his brothers and sisters would say, "There goes our Abbott, the Cravett with the great habit of inventing important things."

A Valentine for My Easter Basket

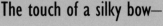

The crinkle of see-through cellophane—

The touch of a silky bow—

The jelly beans buried in make-believe grass—

Easter basket, I love you so!

The chocolate bunny tucked inside—

Soft marshmallow chicks in a row—

The magic you bring to this April day—

Easter basket, I love you so!

— Bobbi Katz

Patchwork Basket

This basket is designed to use scrap materials. Adapt directions to what you have available. The Patchwork Basket can be a spring gift basket or an Easter basket.

MATERIALS

1 cardboard moving box, at least 24 inches wide, cut into 5 pieces:

1 piece 10 x 14 inches (for bottom)

2 pieces 5 x 24 inches, cut so ridges run across short side (for sides)

2 pieces 2 x 24 inches, cut so ridges run across short side (for handles)

Tape

Stapler

Water

White glue

30 pieces newsprint or scrap paper, cut into 2 x 6-inch strips (cut a few at a time)

Wrapping paper, wallpaper, comic paper, origami paper, and/or almost any colorful lightweight paper cut as follows:

20 or more pieces cut into geometric shapes, each approximately 3 to 4 inches in diameter

25 pieces cut into 1 x 3-inch strips (for grass)

1 #14 (1-inch) paintbrush

Scissors

3 2-inch squares of lightweight plastic

Hole punch

STEPS

1. *Bottom:* Have an adult help you cut the bottom piece so that the corners are rounded.

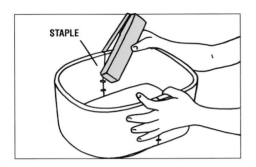

2. *Sides:* Wrap side pieces around the outside of the bottom. Glue or tape as you go. Staple the sides where they overlap each other at each end.

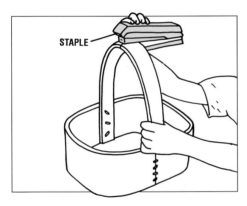

3. *Handle:* Staple a handle piece inside the basket in the middle of each side wall. Curve the handle pieces up and overlap them onto each other. Staple where they overlap.

4. *Mix water and glue:* Mix equal amounts of water and glue in a small bowl. Start with ½ cup of each and repeat as needed.

5. *Dip strips and apply:* Dip a 2 x 6-inch paper strip in the glue mixture, then run it between two fingers to remove excess

glue. Apply strip randomly on basket inside or outside. Repeat with other strips, overlapping as you go. Smooth surface with your hands. Let basket dry 8 hours.

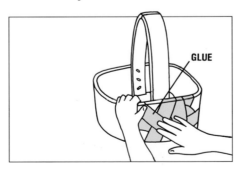

6. *Apply colored paper:* Carefully paint a small area on the basket with the glue mixture and apply one of the geometric pieces of paper. Repeat this, overlapping the pieces. Cover the entire basket inside and out. Let dry 4 hours.

7. *Curl grass and make confetti:* Take a 1 x 3-inch grass strip and run it along the edge of a table or a dull pair of children's scissors to curl it. Repeat with other pieces. Place curled grass inside basket. With hole punch, make confetti from the colored plastic. Sprinkle the plastic confetti into grass in basket.

CHAPTER FIVE

Baby Easter Animals

Many baby animals are born in the spring around the time of Easter. Clumsy little lambs and baby colts try over and over to stand on their wobbly, skinny legs. Finally, they are up and, after a few tumbles, frolicking in the fields. The eggs that the mother hens have been sitting on start to move as fuzzy chicks peck at the inside of their shells. They push their way out into the world with peeps and cheeps. Baby bunnies look like tiny fur balls. Soon they open their eyes and learn to thump their feet and hop about.

Long ago in Egypt, people regarded the birth of a chicken as a small miracle. But really, all baby animals are a source of wonder to everyone who sees them. They are new life, a sign of new beginnings, just like the season of Spring and Easter. There are pictures of baby animals on Easter cards, we read about them in stories, and our Easter candy is shaped like them.

In Los Angeles, the Blessing of the Animals takes place on the Saturday before Easter at the old Plaza Church. Children bring pets of all kinds, from cats and dogs to llamas and canaries, and create a procession into the plaza. On a platform decorated with flowers, a priest blesses the animals as they pass by.

Of all the Easter animals, the lamb plays the largest part in the Easter story. This began about two thousand years ago when Christians called Jesus the "Lamb of God." People called Jesus this for many reasons, but mostly because he was as gentle as a lamb.

In some countries, lamb-shaped pastries and butter shaped as a lamb are part of the Easter table. In Finland, Easter lambs are made of wax and are supposed to have magic powers, and children wear lamb charms of gold or silver around their necks. In Italy and Czechoslovakia, cakes are made in the shape of

Twelve New Chicks

"No, no, no," said the clucking hen;
"I've something else to do;
I'm busy sitting on our eggs,
I cannot walk with you."

The clucking hen sat on her nest,
She made it on the hay;
And warm and snug beneath her breast
A dozen white eggs lay.

Crack, crack, went all the eggs,
Out popped the chickens small;
"Cluck," said the clucking hen,
"Now I can see you all."

"Come along, my little chicks,
I'll take a walk with you."
"Hello!" said their father.
"Cock-a-doodle-do!"

—Anonymous

The Squirrel

Whisky, frisky

Hippity hop,

Up he goes

To the Treetop!

Whirly, twirly,

Round and round,

Down he scampers

To the ground.

Furly, curly,

What a tail!

Tall as a feather,

Broad as a sail!

Where's his supper?

In the shell,

Snappity, crackity,

Out it fell!

— Anonymous

A Little Bird

A little bird sits in the willow;

A little song sings he;

He nods his head, he taps his foot,

All in the willow tree!

lambs. In Sicily, lamb-shaped candies made of spun sugar are a special treat.

Years ago, shepherds and farmers thought the lamb was a sign of good luck. It was said that a lamb seen at Easter would bring a whole year of good fortune. If you see a lamb on Easter Sunday, it is very good luck indeed—especially if the lamb is looking in your direction! Be sure to smile back, wave, and shout, "Happy Easter," and maybe, just maybe, you will have a year of more fun, more happiness, and lots of sunshine!

Mary Had A Little Lamb

Mary had a little lamb,

Its fleece was white as snow;

And everywhere that Mary went,

The lamb was sure to go.

It followed her to school one day,

Which was against the rule;

It made the children laugh and play,

To see a lamb in school.

— Sarah J. Hale and John Roulstone

The poem "Mary Had a Little Lamb" was about a real lamb who followed Mary Sawyer to the Redstone School House in Massachusetts, about 1820.

At the Blessing of the Animals in 1983, Maria Alonzo did not have a pet to take to the service because she was not allowed to have one in the apartment where she and her family lived. But this did not keep Maria from taking something to be blessed. She took her favorite stuffed animal, Poco the pig. The priest didn't mind at all.

One female cottontail bunny can give birth to as many as thirty babies a year. Newly born cottontails look a lot like baby kittens.

Baby squirrels are born furless and blind, but in six weeks, they are almost as quick and strong as their mothers.

Baby Lettuce Salad

There are small heads of lettuce in the vegetable section of most markets. These are called baby lettuce. Their leaves are soft and tasty. A new bunny rabbit would love eating something like this if it could. You will, too.

INGREDIENTS FOR 6 SERVINGS

4 oz. goat cheese (if you don't like goat cheese, substitute mozzarella cheese)

2 heads baby lettuce

3 pears

2 tablespoons chopped dried apricots

¼ cup quartered walnuts

INGREDIENTS FOR 1 CUP SWEET AND SOUR DRESSING

½ cup sour cream

¼ cup orange juice

1 tablespoon sugar

¼ teaspoon ground cinnamon

¼ teaspoon paprika

pinch salt

1. Crumble goat cheese, or grate mozzarella, on a plate and let sit to reach room temperature.

2. Rinse baby lettuce (the leaves are small enough that you will not need to tear them). Set leaves on paper towels to drain.

3. Core pears, but leave peel on. Slice pears, long ways, into 8 pieces each.

4. Divide lettuce evenly onto 6 salad plates.

5. Arrange 4 pear pieces on top of each plate of lettuce and sprinkle cheese, apricots, and walnuts on top.

6. Beat all dressing ingredients in a bowl until smooth. Chill until ready to drizzle over salad.

7. Drizzle 2 tablespoons of dressing over each serving.

The Bunnies All Sleep Soundly

The bunnies all sleep soundly,
Beneath the moon's bright ray;
They nod their heads together,
And dream the night away.

— Anonymous

Easter Lamb

BY MARY ROBINSON
FROM THE STORY BY ANNE D. KYLE

Cathy hurried to the field where she and her father kept a flock of sheep. The lambs were frolicking and tussling with each other. Cathy called three times, then watched with delight as the little fat-tailed lamb named Sophie ran toward her.

The lamb nuzzled Cathy's legs and bleated softly at her. But Cathy's excitement quickly changed to sadness. "Oh, Sophie, how am I going to save you from being sold? You weren't supposed to be my pet but I couldn't help myself."

She cuddled the lamb and fought back tears. She remembered the first letter she'd sent to her best friend: "Dear Annie, Spending a year on a sheep farm is going to be fun. I love it. Dad lets me take care of the lambs and there's one that's my favorite. She is *so* cute. Dad's warned me not to get attached to the lambs because eventually they are going to be sold. Of course I'd never do that. . . ."

"Boy, was I wrong," thought Cathy. "Easter is a week from this Sunday and it's going to be the worst Easter of my life." Sophie was going to be sold this weekend unless Cathy did something fast. Her only hope was to try once again to persuade her father to let her keep the lamb. She wiped tears off her cheeks when she heard him coming up the path.

"Hi, Dad, I want to talk to you about Sophie."

"Cathy, I told you it's not a good idea to name the lamb. She's not a playmate. You know she's going to be sold."

"But—"

"No buts. I agreed to let you help take care of the lambs and you promised you'd do your part."

Cathy sighed. "That promise is impossible to keep."

Her dad's voice softened. "I know you love Soph—uh—the lamb, but you agreed."

Cathy's throat tightened and she couldn't answer. She looked across the field. A hawk, high against the sky, soared and wheeled, then hung motionless. Nearby, a squirrel scampered to a tree, stared at her for a moment, then ran up the trunk. Cathy wished she could scamper away like that with Sophie.

"You're really going to sell her?" she asked.

Her father put his arm around her shoulder. "I appreciate how hard this is for you. But try to remember that we can't always have everything we want."

"I'll try."

He hugged her. "Good. I'll see you after school."

Cathy watched until her father's tall, lean form was obscured by the trees. She led

Sophie to the woodshed in back of the house they were renting. Sophie's eyes seemed to look at her so beseechingly that Cathy cried as she closed the gate. Then she ran to the house to get ready to go to school.

Cathy raced home from school as fast as she could and ran to play with Sophie. She called softly as she approached the fence. No answer came back. She called again. Still no answer. The gate was open and swinging creakily. She raced across to the woodshed. Sophie was gone!

Now what was she going to do? Obviously she hadn't latched the gate securely and her father would think she'd let Sophie escape on purpose. Cathy's mind raced. What if she couldn't find Sophie? Why couldn't the lamb be free?

Unfortunately, Cathy knew the answer. The lamb was too young to be on her own. But maybe Cathy could find her and feed her secretly until she was old enough. But as Cathy thought about how she would do that, she realized there would be problems, the worst of which was lying to her father. Gradually, Cathy came to the only possible solution: she had to find Sophie—and fast. Her father would be coming anytime.

Cathy slipped through the gate and tried to imagine where Sophie would go. She followed the path past the trees and past the field. She headed into the brush and called frequently. But she had no luck finding Sophie.

After a while, the path narrowed and became steeper. Cathy's father had warned her not to walk beyond this point: "You must not be alone out there. It isn't safe." But what could she do? If it wasn't safe for her, it was even more dangerous for Sophie. Cathy had to go on. "Besides, Sophie can't be much further," she reassured herself.

Cathy walked more slowly, for the path had progressed along a ridge. The path was

narrow and rocky, crumbling off to craggy ledges below. Soon her father would realize she was gone and then what would she do? She sat down to rest and think. Suddenly, she heard a plaintive "Baa-a." Cathy called loudly back. She heard another "Baa-a." This time Cathy figured out where it came from.

She crept to the edge of the steep bank. Below, midway between safety and danger, on a broad rock half in sun and half in shadow, was a fat-tailed little lamb. Sophie!

The lamb lay stretched within the protecting shade, her tiny sides heaving. She struggled to her feet and attempted small steps along the rock, bleating for help.

"Here I am, Sophie," yelled Cathy. "Up here."

Sophie looked upward along the hillside until she saw Cathy, then bleated hopefully.

Cathy thought about how she was going to get down to Sophie. She was only about ten feet down, but it was a very treacherous ten feet.

Cathy carefully traced a path along roots, rocks, and ledges. When she'd satisfied herself that the route was manageable, she swung her leg over the edge.

"Wait! Wait!"

It was her father. "I can't. I'm sorry, Dad. Sophie needs me."

"I'll help you," shouted her father. In seconds he was next to her, mumbling, "I was so worried, so worried."

"I had to find Sophie. I—"

"We'll talk about that later." He looked over the edge. "Ah, so there's the little one." Her father smiled, then said firmly, "You did a good job finding her. Now let's work together. I'm taller. I'll climb down and you can lift her out of my arms."

Cathy nodded. She lay on her stomach, her head and shoulders over the edge, while her father climbed down slowly, reassuring Sophie as he approached her. After he had her, he climbed quickly to within reach of Cathy's outstretched arms.

Cathy clasped Sophie to her chest and rolled back to safety. Soon her father joined them. Cathy cradled Sophie in her lap.

"We'd better go or Mom will be worried," said her father. He carried Sophie and let her nestle against his chest.

"Dad, it must have been my fault that Sophie got out and I worried you'd think I did it on purpose."

Her father took her hand. "I was worried that you'd run away."

"Dad, I'd never do that!"

They laughed and walked quietly for a while.

"But what about Sophie?" asked Cathy.

"Don't worry. I did a lot of thinking while I was looking for you. Since Sophie's that important to you, I think she needs to stay with us awhile. I like your suggestion of joining the 4H club. You can learn a lot from taking care of her."

"Oh, Dad, I'll work hard in the club. You'll be proud of me. I might even win a ribbon."

"I'm proud of you now, Cathy."

Sophie bleated softly as if she, too, agreed.

"Thank you, Dad," said Cathy, hugging him. "This is going to be the best Easter I've ever had."

Mechanical Chickadee

In spring, baby chicks break out of their shells. They stretch and wobble around. They try their beaks and flap their wings. This mechanical chickadee also moves its beak and flap its wings.

Hole punch

Orange marker or paint

Glue

12 yellow feathers

Glitter

Large blunt needle

2 small brass brads

4 yellow ⅜-inch wooden beads

Tape for cloth paper

2 yards ⅛-inch satin ribbon

2 ½-inch wiggly eyes

STEPS

1. *Trace:* Trace pattern on poster board and cut all pieces out. Mark one side of each piece "back." Punch holes where shown. Have an adult help you cut slot for beak where shown.

2. *Color and glue:* Color legs and back orange. Set beak aside and glue legs to back of body at the bottom. Let glue dry.

MATERIALS

1 8½ x 11-inch piece yellow posterboard or card stock

Scissors

Pencil

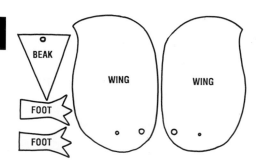

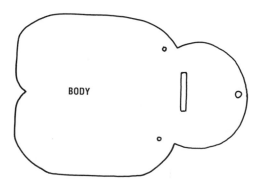

3. *Glue and dry:* Glue feathers on top edge of wings. Let dry.

4. *Glue glitter:* Squeeze a small amount of glue where you want glitter. Sprinkle glitter on body. Let dry and shake off loose glitter.

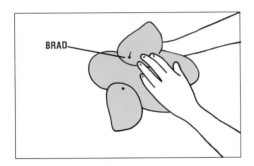

5. *Attach:* Attach wings by first poking through the larger hole with needle where shown. Then, push brad through with head in front. Punch brad through hole on wing against back side of body. Place a wooden bead on the brad. Bend arms of brad to secure the wing and bead. Do not tighten brads so much that wings will not flap easily.

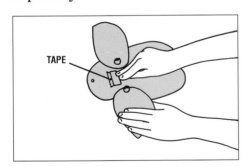

6. *Slide:* Slide beak into slot from the back side with beak pointing down until it stops. The beak slot is smaller than the beak and will hold it in place. Tape beak on back side underneath slot, overlapping onto beak—tape should be only as wide as slot or beak will not operate.

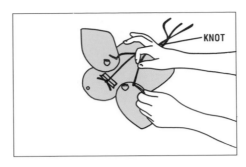

7. *Thread and tie:* Cut 3 18-inch pieces of ribbon. Thread one piece ribbon through the hole in beak. Tie ribbon into a knot. Repeat with the other two ribbon pieces, threading them through the holes in wings.

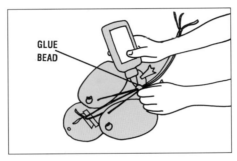

8. *Carve:* Have an adult help you carve off a flat area of one bead (a flat side will stick much better than a round one), and glue the flat side to the middle of the lower back of body. Let dry.

9. *Thread:* Thread the 3 ribbons through the bead. Keep the bird's wings down while you work. It is important that the 3 ribbons are equally tight. You may need to work at this to get it right.

10. *Tie:* Thread the 3 ribbons through another bead 9 inches below your bird. Tie here with a feather. This should secure all 3 ribbons so that when you pull on them, they all move together.

11. *Cut and tie:* Cut the remaining piece of ribbon in half. Tie one of these pieces in a bow around the bead, feather, and 3 ribbons below bird.

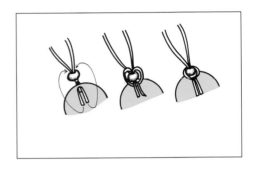

12. *Tie:* The other ribbon goes through the hole punched in the head and allows you to hang your bird on the wall. To do this, bring the two ends through a wooden bead. Secure it here by tying a knot. Bring both loose ends of this ribbon through the hole in head and loop back through. Glue ends to back of head.

13. *Try and adjust:* Hold bird in midair and pull on the 3 ribbons at bottom of your chickadee. This should make the wings and beak rise. Adjust where necessary by loosening or tightening ribbons. Add a feather to the top head bead. Glue on wiggly eyes.

CHAPTER SIX

A Dozen Eggs

The egg is one of the oldest symbols of spring. Inside is the miracle of new life. When the little chick hatches, it reminds people of the return of life in springtime.

Since ancient times, the egg has symbolized the universe, perhaps because they are similar in shape. One legend tells of a large egg that was made of chaos. The chaos split the egg's shell and created two separate parts. The bottom part became the earth and the upper part formed the sky.

Long ago, people in India, Egypt, and Greece believed the universe was hatched from an egg. They called this egg the "cosmic egg" or the "world egg."

The Samoan people, who live on the Samoan Islands in the South Pacific, believed that their great god Tangaloa-Langi (TAN-ga-loh-a LAN-ee) hatched out of an egg and that the islands they live on were created from bits of the shells that were scattered across the Pacific Ocean.

Perhaps the oldest springtime custom is the giving and receiving of eggs. As far back as 1290, Edward I gave hundreds of eggs to the members of his household and to his servants. In Germany and Austria, people gave each other green eggs on Maundy Thursday, the Thursday before Easter, also called "Green Thursday." The German word for "mourning," which means being sad, is related to the word for green. Because Christians were mourning for Jesus on this day, they gave green eggs and ate green foods, and priests wore green robes.

The Germans also created the Easter Egg Tree many years ago, probably as a reminder of the Christmas tree tradition. To make lightweight ornaments for the tree, they pricked small holes in the ends of egg shells and blew out the insides. Then they colored the hollow shells and hung them from the branches of a tree or bush outside. You can see these Easter trees

This Little Piggie Went to the Market
(Old Mexican version)

(Grab a friend's toe as you say each line, starting with the big one. On the last line, tickle the foot.)

This one stole an egg,

this one fried it,

this one salted it,

this one ate it,

and this old rabbit went

and tattled all about it!

Hickety, Pickety, My Black Hen

Hickety, pickety, my black hen,
She lays eggs for gentlemen;
Gentlemen come every day
To see what my black hen doth lay.

Easter Eggs

I gather the eggs each day for my
mamma

Wherever an egg can be found,

In the nests in the hen house, the cow
shed and manger,

And sometimes there's one on the
ground.

I climb the hay-loft and hunt in the
corners,

Where the old biddies hid them away,

Snuggled back in a nest where no one
can see them

They lay them up there in the hay.

I follow the turkeys way down in the
meadows

Where they think that no one will go,

But wherever they hid them, I always
can find them,

Their cute tricks I every one know.

But hunt as I will, it is only at Easter

The nest of the rabbit I find

With its eggs many colored, blue,
green, red, and yellow

The best of all eggs to my mind.

—**Anonymous**

today in many parts of America.

During Lent, the Ukrainians and other Slavic people decorate eggs in mosaic-like patterns. These are called *pysanky* (pee-ZAHN-kee) eggs. Pysanky is a dye method that uses wax. First, fine lines of symbols and intricate patterns are drawn on the eggshell—the symbol of the sun stands for good fortune, a rooster or hen means fulfillment of wishes, a stag or deer is for good health, and flowers represent love and charity. Then, hot wax is applied to the areas that are to be left natural egg color. Next, the egg is dipped in the lightest color dye, usually yellow. When the dye dries, more wax is applied to the areas that are to be left yellow. This process is repeated, dipping the egg into a darker dye each time. The result is a beautifully patterned and colored egg.

Russians traditionally made gifts of eggs at Easter, having them blessed by the priest before giving them as presents. But the Fabergé (fab-uhr-ZHAY) eggs were even more special. In 1881 a jeweler by the name of Karl Fabergé was asked by Tsar Alexander III to make an egg decorated with precious jewels as an Easter surprise for the tsarina, Maria Fydorovna (fee-dor-OH vna). Tsarina Maria was so thrilled with her gift that Mr. Fabergé made an egg each Easter for her. Each one was a masterpiece, decorated with real jewels on the outside and inside. And they all contained a surprise jewel or miniature model inside. Some of the eggs were designed so you could see the wonders of the inside immediately; others had to be opened to expose the tiny scene inside. One particularly famous Fabergé egg is the Resurrection Egg, which was made in 1889. It can be seen at the Forbes Museum in New York City. Many of the other Fabergé eggs can also be found in museums.

Another Easter custom in many countries is eating eggs. Thousands of years ago, Greeks ate roasted eggs, while the Romans thought that starting a special meal with an egg would bring them luck. The eggs were blessed by the priest in honor of the Resurrection of Jesus Christ. Today, in Scandinavian countries everyone tries to eat as many eggs as possible on Easter morning. The Danish people eat theirs dipped in mustard sauce. Italians bake whole eggs in loaves of bread.

An exciting part of Easter today are the Easter Egg hunts. In grassy fields, backyards, and even living rooms, eggs are hidden by grown-ups (or is it the Easter Bunny?) for children to find. The most famous of these is the one held at the White House in Washington, D.C. Hundreds of children scramble to find not only eggs, but packages of jelly beans and plastic egg shapes filled with prizes.

Egg in the Eye with Green Tomato Salsa

This is a fun recipe that uses eggs. First, cook the salsa, leaving the juices from the tomato in the pan. When you add the bread to the juices, they will give it a tangy flavor.

**INGREDIENTS FOR
2 EGGS IN THE EYE WITH SALSA**

*1 medium-green tomato or
tomatillo*

3 tablespoons butter

*2 ½-inch-thick slices
multigrain bread*

2 eggs

*½ cup grated gouda or
mozzarella cheese*

1. Dice the tomato into tiny pieces.

2. In frying pan, melt 1 tablespoon butter over medium heat.

3. Add diced tomato and cook until almost transparent.

4. Set tomato salsa aside. Do not clean the pan.

5. Cut a round or oval-shaped hole in the middle of each bread slice with a round cookie cutter or knife.

6. In the same frying pan used for the tomatoes, melt 1 tablespoon butter over medium heat.

7. Add 1 slice bread. Heat on one side for 2 minutes.

8. Crack open 1 egg and pour in the hole.

9. Heat this 1 minute more, then turn over with spatula.

10. Heat on this side 1 minute, or until clear part of egg turns white.

11. Add grated cheese to top. Heat 1 more minute and remove from the pan.

12. Using the remaining butter, bread, and egg, repeat steps 5 through 11 to make the second Egg in the Eye.

13. Serve Eggs in the Eye with Tomato Salsa spooned over the top.

Eric's Excellent Easter Adventure

BY SHERI BROWNRIGG AND MARY ROBINSON

Since he was a very little boy, Eric loved the Easter Bunny more than any other holiday figure, including Santa Claus. He loved how cute and cuddly and soft he imagined the Easter Bunny to be. He loved the basket overflowing with goodies that the Easter Bunny left for him.

When his mother asked Eric what he wanted to be for Halloween, he knew immediately. The Easter Bunny! So she made a fuzzy suit with long floppy ears and a fat cotton tail. Since then, Eric's greatest wish was that the Easter Bunny would need help delivering baskets and would take Eric with him. So, early Easter Eve, Eric put on his Easter Bunny suit. He sat by the window in his room, watching. He wished with all his might that the Easter Bunny would come.

His mother came in and said, "How wonderful you look. I'm sure when the Easter Bunny sees you, he'll want you to help him. Hop into bed. I'll wake you when he comes."

Eric put his head on his pillow, being careful not to crush his ears, closed his eyes, and repeated his wish with all his might. "Please let the Easter Bunny come get me. Please let the Easter Bunny come get me. . . ." Suddenly he felt a little tickle on his cheek. There, with long wispy whiskers and a wiggly nose, was the Easter Bunny!

The Easter Bunny looked just as Eric had imagined, only he was taller, softer, had longer ears, a pinker nose, and wonderfully long whiskers. He brushed Eric's hair off his forehead.

"Well, my boy, I hear you want to be my helper."

Eric gasped and sputtered.

"Does that mean yes?" asked the Easter Bunny.

"Oh, yes," said Eric. He couldn't believe his wish was actually coming true. "Oh, please, please, take me with you."

"That's why I'm here. C'mon, we have to go. We have lots of work to do."

There in the middle of the street was what looked like a gigantic pink sugar Easter Egg. Yellow icing crisscrossed all over it, and in the middle of the X's were pink rosebuds with sprigs of purple hyacinth. In front of the egg, dozens of rows of yellow ducks in a licorice harness stood at attention.

"What's this?" asked Eric.

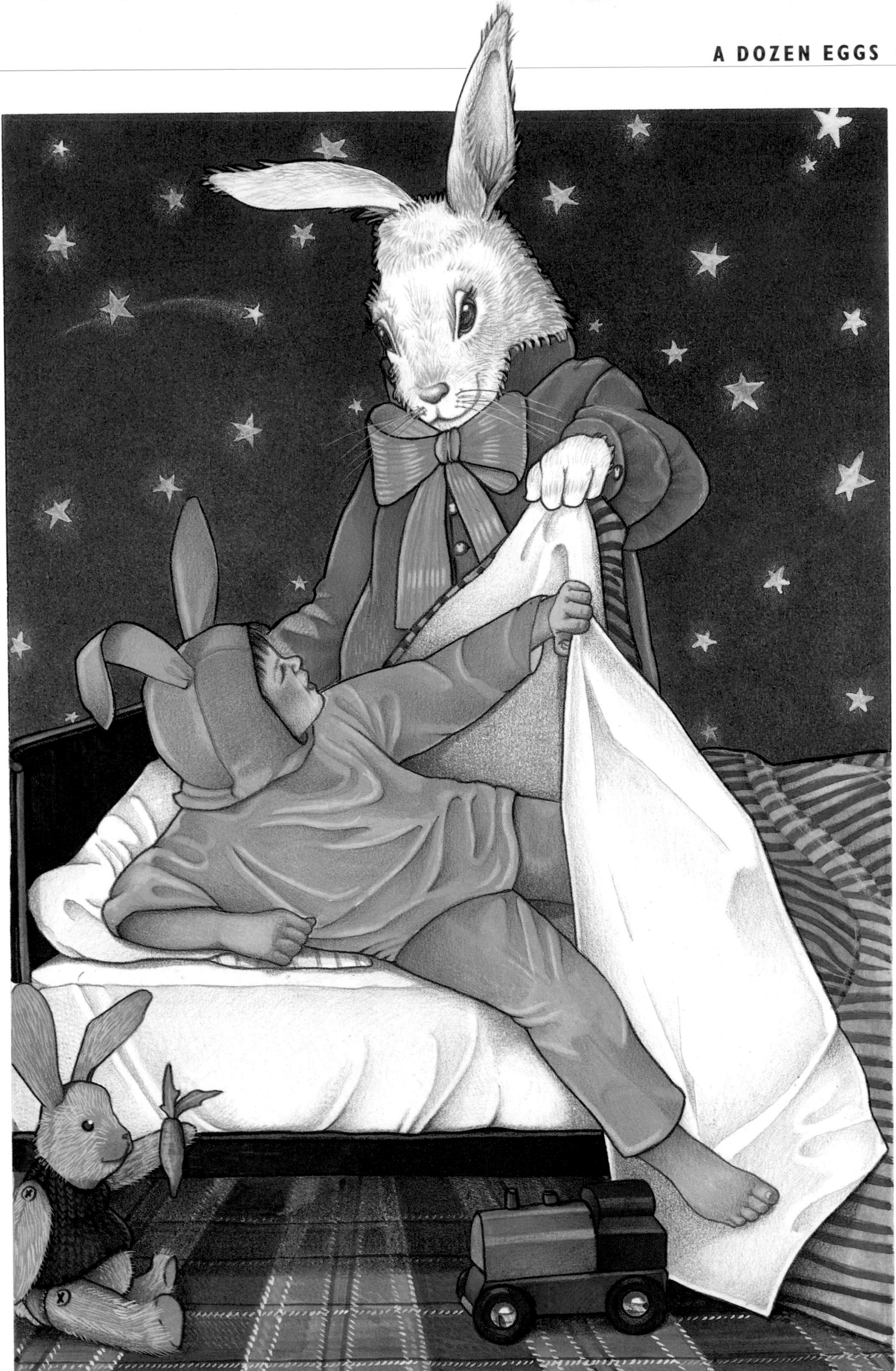

The Easter Bunny waved his paw and a turquoise-blue hatch door opened. "The Cosmic Egg. Climb aboard."

Eric's eyes opened wide. The outside of the egg looked like a beautiful Easter Egg, but inside everything was incredibly high-tech.

"Wow!" he said. "I didn't know you delivered Easter eggs in a spaceship."

"No one knows—except you," said the Easter Bunny. "It'll be our secret. I know I can trust you. You're my helper."

"But what about the ducks?" asked Eric.

"I use them for ground transport only." The Easter Bunny pushed two gold buttons. A bronze hatch silently opened. The ducks waddled and quacked in to their quarters.

The Easter Bunny pulled a purple lever and asked Eric to flick a purple switch. Eric watched on the monitor as a blue robin's eggshell encased the Cosmic Egg.

Noticing the puzzled expression on Eric's face, the Easter Bunny explained, "The cover protects the sugar flowers, and enables us to enter hyperspace."

"Hyperspace? What about the Easter Eggs and goodies?" He hoped they weren't going to be cosmic, too.

"Don't worry. They're made with the same traditional designs and recipes. But I've become computerized. And I have networks of workers all over the galaxy on different planets. Soon you'll understand." The Easter Bunny looked Eric up and down. "By the way, that's a great bunny suit."

Eric's head was spinning with excitement and so was the Cosmic Egg. On the monitor he could see Earth receding in the distance. Then the Cosmic Egg roared through space, swerving around satellites and dodging meteors.

Soon the Easter Bunny shouted, "First stop: Planet Basket."

Planet Basket had baskets of straw, wicker, cat tail, pine needles, and grass. Some were colored, some were natural. "Eric, you and the ducks can help me load these."

Thank goodness baskets are light and easy to carry.

"Now, Planet Grass," the Easter Bunny said.

Looking out the window, Eric saw pink and green plastic grass, real yellow grass, and even neon orange grass.

"Load it up," the Easter Bunny said. And they stuffed the baskets.

"Where next?" Eric asked.

"Planet Chocolate, of course."

"Mmmmm," said Eric. "Sounds good to me."

When they landed, the hatch opened and Eric stepped out into a chocolate extravaganza. As far as he could see there were stacks and stacks of chocolate Easter goodies: chocolate bunnies, chocolate chicks, and chocolate eggs. They were arranged by size from extra small to jumbo, the hollow ones in front and the solid goodies in back.

After they loaded the last chocolate piece, Eric asked, "Now for Planet Jelly Bean?"

"No, we pick those out of the atmosphere. You can put a few in your pocket if you wish."

Sure enough, there were jelly beans floating in outer space—peanut butter flavor, lemon-lime, and root beer. It was like catching stars.

"Last stop before we start our deliveries is Planet Marshmallow," Easter Bunny said.

There they picked up all the marshmallow chicks and eggs.

"That ought to do it," the Easter Bunny said, as the hatch closed. "Now we have to make all the deliveries to the children." The Easter Bunny pressed a silver button, turned a gold knob until it pointed to "Deliveries," then pulled three lemon levers. Everything started moving super fast. Baskets were put together. Bows were added to the top, and the deliveries began. Faster than fast, the Cosmic Egg stopped at every child's house in every country that wished for the Easter Bunny.

Eric was impressed. Now he understood that Easter Bunny had to be high-tech to accomplish his job. After the last delivery was made, Eric fell asleep. He was exhausted.

The Easter Bunny keyed in the command for sending the Cosmic Egg to Eric's neighborhood. Within minutes, the Easter Bunny dropped Eric gently in his bed. Eric woke up just enough to hear the Easter Bunny say, "Thank you for all your help. You were terrific. See you next year. And don't forget our secret."

The next morning Eric found the biggest, best Easter basket he had ever gotten. It was overflowing with all his favorite goodies. And on the top was a huge sugar replica of the Cosmic Egg.

When his mother saw it she exclaimed, "Why you must have a special connection with the Easter Bunny to get such a wonderful basket."

"I do, I do," said Eric.

"When did that happen?"

"Last night," said Eric excitedly. "The Easter Bunny let me help make deliveries."

"What an extraordinary adventure," said his mother, hugging him. "And what's in that fancy sugar egg with the pink rosebuds and yellow crisscrosses?"

"Oh, that." Eric picked up the Cosmic Egg and closed the turquoise hatch. "That's a secret—between me and the Easter Bunny."

"I see," said his mother with an understanding smile.

"Wait," said Eric. He reached in his pocket, pulled out a lemon-lime jelly bean and offered it to her. "I can share this. I got it on my adventure."

His mother ate the jelly bean and exclaimed, "Why this jelly bean is excellent!"

"Just like my Easter," said Eric. And he knew he would never forget his excellent Easter adventure.

Egg Globe

Long ago, some people thought the world began as an egg. Here, you can make a globe in the shape of an egg.

The art of balancing eggs is an ancient Chinese ritual. To do this on the spring equinox is very good luck. On March 20, 1984, a man in New York City celebrated spring by standing thirty eggs upright, exactly balanced on the end, for fifteen minutes. Perhaps you can beat this record. (Ask your mom or dad before you try.)

MATERIALS

1 11-inch balloon

Scissors

1 roll plaster gauze

Water

2 oz. blue acrylic paint

1 #10 round-tipped paintbrush

Pencil

2 oz. green acrylic paint

1 #6 round-tipped paintbrush

Black permanent marker or black paint

Black cord or fishing wire

Molly bolt or hook

STEPS

1. *Blow and tie:* Blow up balloon, but not too full. Tie it.

2. *Measure and cut:* Cut 1 yard of plaster gauze. Cut this into 3-inch pieces. You can cut more later when you see how much more you need.

3. *Dip and squeeze:* Dip one piece plaster gauze in water. With your fingers, gently squeeze out the extra water before you put it on the balloon.

8. *Paint:* Paint the inside of your continents with the green color. Use the #10 brush for the middle areas and the #6 brush for close to the lines. Let dry about 10 minutes. Outline the land with the black marker or paint. Let dry.

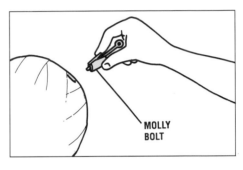

MOLLY BOLT

9. *Tie and bolt:* With a nail or pencil, poke a hole in the top of your globe. Tie black cord or fishing wire to the molly bolt and slip bolt inside the hole, letting the bolt expand to stay inside the balloon. Hang your globe by the cord or wire.

Save a few gauze pieces to do this later. Let plaster dry about 15 minutes.

5. *Pop and cut:* Pop the balloon. Cut off the tied part of balloon if it is sticking out. Plaster over the hole and let dry about 15 minutes.

6. *Paint:* Paint the whole egg blue using the #10 brush. Let paint dry about 10 minutes.

7. *Draw:* With pencil, draw on continents. You don't have to be exact; in fact, you can even make up your own land shapes.

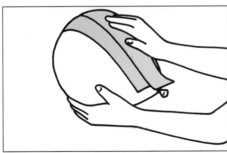

4. *Apply:* Carefully apply gauze to balloon by flattening the piece and smoothing with your hands. Repeat with another plaster piece, overlapping the first by about 1 inch. Cover the entire balloon with plaster gauze in this manner. You won't be able to cover the part where the balloon is tied yet.

An Easter Jingle

With bits of stick and wisps of hay

I've made a little nest;

I've chosen from my Easter eggs

The ones that I like best;

And now I'll get the old white hen

And set her on all six;

So she'll hatch out some red and blue

And pink and yellow chicks.

— Harriet Brewer Sterling

CHAPTER SEVEN

Fun Buns

When you think of Easter, you probably think of some fun things to eat, such as jelly beans, marshmallow chicks, or chocolate eggs. Before these things became traditional treats, children looked forward to wonderful baked breads at Easter. This fun bun custom goes back thousands and thousands of years.

Food has an important place in Easter celebrations because many years ago Christians observed Lent during the forty days before Easter Sunday. During this time they were not allowed to eat meat, milk, eggs, butter, or other fats. In this way, they were reminded that Jesus didn't eat anything during his forty days in the desert. Many Christians today still give up something they really like during this period, such as ice cream or chocolate. It also gives them a chance to get ready for the renewal that starts with Easter.

Long ago, Christians would eat only unleavened bread, bread that is flat because it hasn't risen, during Lent. This bread, made out of flour, water, and salt, is something like a cracker or a pretzel. In fact, pretzels are an old form of Lenten bread.

The first pretzels were made long ago in Rome by monks, men who devote their lives to the church. Monks gave them to poor people who could not afford to buy much food. Pretzels were once called "little arms." If you look closely at the twist of the pretzel, you may see two small arms crossed in prayer.

But when Lent comes to an end and the joyful celebration of the Resurrection begins, the pretzel and the flat, hard Lenten loaves are replaced with fancy breads and spicy buns.

The most famous of these breads are delicious hot-cross buns, an English treat from a time before Easter. Believers offered them as a gift to the spring goddess named Diana in hopes that she would make the spring fruitful. In fact, two tiny hot-cross buns were preserved by volcanic ash in England almost a hundred years before Christ.

In England today on Good Friday (two days before Easter), bakers are very busy at their big, hot ovens. Outside the shops,

Hot Cross-Buns

Hot cross-buns, hot cross-buns,
One a penny, two a penny, hot
  cross-buns;
Smoking hot, piping hot,
Just come out of the baker's shop;
One a penny poke, two a penny tongs,
Three penny fire-shovel, hot cross-buns!

Plum or Plain

A robin and a robin's son
Once went to town to buy a bun.
They couldn't decide on plum or plain
And so they went back home again.

— Anonymous

Bun Yum

Round is my bun, yum, yum!
My pocket's too small
for my bun!
Break it in two! Will that do?
It fits! It fits! Hurrah for you!

Pat-a-Cake, Pat-a-Cake, Baker's Man

Pat-a-cake, pat-a-cake, baker's man!

Make me a cake as fast as you can;

Prick it, and pat it, and mark it with a T,

And put it in the oven for Tommy and me.

Fun Buns

Almost every country has a special bread for Easter.

Some people believe that bread baked on Good Friday will never get moldy.

In some Mexican villages on Palm Sunday, villagers decorate large crosses with baked breads.

Portugal has an Easter cake called <u>folar</u> (fo-LAR). It is round, flat, and sweet, and decorated with hard-boiled eggs.

A traditional Easter cake in Russia is called <u>koulich</u> (KOO-leech).

In parts of Ireland people eat "golden bread," which is similar to French toast.

A favorite Polish pastry for Easter is called <u>mazurek</u> (MAZ-ur-ek). This is a very sweet cake made with honey, nuts, and fruit.

customers stand in line before the doors are open, waiting to enjoy the best and freshest of these sweet raisin rolls with a white cross of icing on their rounded tops. In the streets, sellers with plates shout the hot-cross bun jingle. Children thought that having a hot-cross bun on Good Friday, even though Lent was not over yet, would bring them good luck. The buns were also thought to be charms against sickness and accidents.

In other countries of Europe, many kinds of Easter bread and Easter cake are made. Some are eaten just before Lent starts, on Shrove Tuesday, as a last treat before the Lenten fast begins. The Shrovetide buns of Norway and Denmark are hung from the ceiling, and children try to jump up and take bites out of them while the buns swing crazily on strings. German and Austrian children, on the other hand, would more likely be eating "fast-nachts" (FASHT-nahkts), which taste like doughnuts but are long and twisted.

In Italy, an Easter cake called *ciambella* (chom-BEL-la) is baked. It is made of a crispy dough and shaped either in the form of a dove, for girls, or a horse, for boys. An Easter egg is baked inside and the cake is stuck full of feathers. Although ciambellai are not baked in many bakeries today, many other kinds of Easter cakes still are made, such as colomba di Pasqua (co-LOHM-ba dee PAH-squa), which means "Easter dove," a cake with wings decorated with balls of almond paste and a body twisted to make the bird look as if it is flying.

The Greeks have a festive braid called *tsoureki* (TOO-re-ki). The dough is wrapped around colorful hard-boiled eggs. The Greeks also make a holiday loaf called *christopsomo* (cris-TOPE-so-mo), which is designed with a beautiful cross on top.

On Easter Sunday in the old days, Russians ate Easter cakes with the letters XB, which meant "Christ is risen," on top. And that, after all, is why Easter is a special time of year for Christians. Today, they have something similar called *paska*.

In some parts of Ireland people eat "Golden Bread," which is similar to French toast. And in Poland they have coffee cakes called *babka* on Easter.

There are almost as many different kinds of Easter breads as there are Easter eggs. Smelling the bread baking, and eating it while it is still warm, is another enjoyable part of the holiday.

Beautifully formed garlands of bread are still offered to the Virgin Mary in the Spanish village of Llanes.

In Denmark on the Monday before Ash Wednesday, children have a day off from school. This is also the day they eat Shrovetide buns.

Pretzels

Pretzels have been around since before the Roman Empire. For the Lenten period, these special breads were made from foods that Christians were allowed to eat. These pretzels had no fat, eggs, or milk in them. The dough was shaped in the form of two arms crossed in prayer. They called these breads "little arms."

INGREDIENTS FOR 24 PRETZELS

1 package yeast

1 ½ cups lukewarm water

1 tablespoon sugar

1 teaspoon salt

4 cups flour

2 tablespoons butter (to grease cookie sheets)

1 egg

1 tablespoon water

⅓ cup coarse salt

1. In a large mixing bowl, add yeast to lukewarm water. Let mixture sit for 5 minutes, until it is bubbly.

2. Add the sugar, salt, and 3 cups of the flour to the yeast mixture. Stir until the ingredients are blended. With your hands or wooden spoon, pull dough from the sides of the bowl and form a ball.

3. Place the dough on a lightly floured tabletop.

4. Dust your hands with flour. Begin kneading the dough by pushing with the palm of one hand while pulling the top of the dough over onto itself with your other hand. Knead in the remaining flour 1 tablespoon at a time. After about 5 minutes, the dough should be smooth and elastic, and not sticking to your hands.

5. Tear the dough into 24 pieces. Roll each into a foot-long stick. Leave the dough in sticks or twist it into crossed arms or any other fun shapes.

6. Preheat oven to 425°F.

7. Grease cookie sheets with a small amount of butter and place pretzels on them. Leave several inches of space between them because the dough will grow as it bakes.

8. In a small bowl, combine the egg with 1 tablespoon of water and mix well. Paint the mixture on each pretzel and sprinkle with coarse salt.

9. Bake pretzels for 20 minutes. Remove from oven and cool on wire racks.

10. Serve straight pretzels sticking up in a glass. Serve twisted pretzels in a bowl. These taste good dipped in mustard.

Elena's Ciambella

BY ANNA MILO UPJOHN

As Elena scampered over the road the town clock struck a quarter to four. Elena had an important engagement. Her mother had sent her to draw a jar of water from the public well outside the town, and on the way back she was to stop at the bakery to get her ciambella, which was to come out of the oven at four.

Now a ciambella is an Easter cake, but it is different from any other cake in the world. It is made of flour and sugar and olive oil, and tastes like a crisp cookie. If you are a girl, yours will be in the form of a dove; if a boy, in the form of a galloping horse, with a handle of twisted dough from mane to tail to carry it by. Whichever it may be, an Easter egg will be baked inside the ciambella, and the cake will be stuck full of downy feathers.

Elena's cake was an unusually large one, in the shape of a dove, of course, with wings and tail feathers and an open beak. It had been brought to the bakery on a tray by Elena's mother, and left to be baked.

As Elena panted up the hill she saw Giuseppa outside the cabane, or hut, helping her mother with the washing. The baby stood in a high, narrow box where he could look on and yet was out of mischief, and there he waved his arms and shouted with excitement.

"Where are you going?" called Giuseppa as Elena passed.

"To get my ciambella," cried Elena. "Have you got yours?"

Giuseppa shook her head. "I'm not going to have any," she said.

"Not this year," added her mother, looking up. "Perhaps next. But we are going to make the cabane clean for Easter."

Elena looked at Giuseppa sympathetically.

"Too bad!" exclaimed Elena. "Well, I must hurry. Ciao [a parting that is pronounced "chow" and means "goodbye"], Giuseppa."

"Ciao, Elena."

When Elena reached the bakery she found a great crowd there. The four o'clock cakes were coming out of the oven. Far back in the glow Elena could see her own ciambella on the stone floor of the oven, larger than all the rest, its feathers waving tantalizingly.

In the midst of the women and children stood the cook, with smooth black hair, huge earrings of gold and pearls that reached to her shoulders, and a clean, flowered kerchief tucked into her corset. She was bare-armed and brown, and held what looked like a great pancake turner with a very long handle. With this she could reach into the depths of the oven, which was as big as a pantry, and scoop out the cakes, even those all the way back.

There were all sorts of cakes, large and small; some were cookies, and some were big loaves made with almonds and honey and eggs. The whole place smelled delicious, and everyone stood on tiptoe to see his or her own cake pulled out of the oven. Finally Elena's ciambella was put into her hands, still hot and fragrant.

Just then a little girl named Letitia came in to ask for coals with which to light the fire at home. The cook raked a few from the oven and put them into the pot of ashes that Letitia carried. Covering them with her apron, Letitia went out with Elena.

"Just look at my ciambella," said Elena proudly, as she carried it carefully in both hands. "Isn't it a beauty!"

"Yes," said Letitia. "I am going to have one, too. It will be baked tomorrow. Of course," she added, "it won't be quite as big as yours, because Maria will have one, and Gino will have a horse. But they'll all taste the same."

"Just think," said Elena. "Giuseppa isn't going to have any!"

"Not any?" cried Letitia. "How dreadful! I never heard of a house without a ciambella! They must be very poor."

"Yes, but at school Giuseppa always has a clean apron and clean hands. Well, ciao, Letitia."

"Ciao, Elena."

The girls parted, and Elena walked proudly through the streets, carrying the cake as though in a procession.

She climbed the outside stair that led to her house, built over the donkey stable. Her mother had gone out to the fountain to polish her pots. The big dim room, with its brown rafters and the dark furniture ranged along the walls, was very quiet.

A patch of sunshine made a bright spot on the stone floor, and in it a white pigeon drowsed. It did not move, even when Elena stepped over it. The little girl looked down and laughed at the comical resemblance between the pigeon and her ciambella; her pigeon sat up very straight and stiff because it had an Easter egg inside.

Elena carefully set the cake on a big chest while she struggled to open the bottom drawer of the bureau. There she laid the cake in a nest of clean aprons and handkerchiefs, to rest until Saturday afternoon, when it would be taken out to be blessed. Not until Sunday morning would its fine feathers be plucked and its crisp wings bitten off.

The next days were very busy. Everyone in Sezze was cleaning house frantically before Easter. Washing hung over every balcony, the yellow and flowered handkerchiefs and aprons making the whole street gay. Every bit of furniture was polished, windows were cleaned, curtains were washed, and floors were scrubbed. Above all, the copper water jars and basins were taken out to the fountains and scoured with lemon and sand.

There was the warmth of spring in the air after a cold winter. On the slopes below the town the almond trees were in blossom, and the snow had disappeared from the mountains, the tops of which were covered with clouds.

Far below the town a fertile plain—the Pontine Marshes—stretched out to the sea. Giuseppa's father worked on the flats, and the family lived in a cabane high up on the mountain, just below the town, where land was cheap. It was true that Giuseppa's father was very poor, but he was also saving his money to build a little stone house to take the place of the cabane. He told the children that when they had the house they should also have a ciambella every year.

In the meantime Giuseppa helped her mother make the cabane as neat as possible for Easter. It was round, with a thatched roof that came to a peak at the top. Inside there was only one room, and that had an earthen floor and no windows. There were no openings except the doors, and no chimney.

When the fire was built on the floor in the middle of the room the smoke struggled up through holes in the roof, but the family lived out in the sun most of the time, and went into the cabane only when it rained or was very cold.

As Elena went back and forth for water those busy days she sometimes looked over the wall and saw Giuseppa hanging clothes on the bushes or beating a mattress, and there was smoke coming through the roof as if water were being heated. Elena felt very sorry for her friend, and every night prayed to God to send Giuseppa a ciambella.

Giuseppa, not knowing this, felt bitter toward Elena and jealous of her great feathered cake. Also, she herself prayed earnestly for a ciambella. On Easter morning she made herself as fine as she could and went to church. She combed back her short hair and laid a white embroidered handkerchief over it. She had small gold earrings and a coral necklace, and she put on a light blue cotton apron and her corn-colored handkerchief with roses over her shoulders.

On her way home Elena came running after her. "Oh, Giuseppa," she asked earnestly, "did you get a ciambella?"

"No, I didn't," said Giuseppa, and passed on.

Elena was much disappointed. She had prayed hard, and felt that a cake should have been sent to Giuseppa. Then suddenly she stopped short in the street. "Why," she said, "perhaps God hasn't got a ciambella, and I have!"

She went home thoughtfully and opened the drawer and looked a long time at her ciambella. After dinner Elena took the cake lovingly in her arms and carried it into the street. It was the last time it would be on parade. She passed the groups of children, all munching ciambella, and made her way to Giuseppa's hut. Giuseppa was outside, feeding the baby from a bowl of bread and milk.

"Happy Easter!" cried Elena.

"Happy Easter!" replied Giuseppa, her eyes fixed on the cake.

"I brought my ciambella to eat with you," said Elena cautiously, "and you may hold it, and oh, Giuseppa, you may have the egg!"

Giuseppa grew scarlet. "I never saw such a beauty," she said. "And what feathers!"

"I stuck them into the dough myself," said Elena. "That is why there are so many."

"Do you know," said Giuseppa shyly, "I prayed for a ciambella."

"And you got it!" cried Elena triumphantly.

Bread Dough Dove

These doves are similar to the *colomba di Pasqua* from Italy. You can make six 6-inch doves with this recipe. And even though this is a craft, you can actually eat the doves if you want to.

MATERIALS

1 package active dry yeast

¼ cup lukewarm water

¾ cup butter, softened

½ cup sugar

⅓ cup lukewarm milk

½ teaspoon salt

5 eggs

5 to 5 ½ cups all-purpose flour

1 egg, beaten with 1 tablespoon water

STEPS

1. *Dissolve:* Dissolve yeast in water in a large mixing bowl. Set aside for 5 minutes.

2. *Blend:* Stir butter, sugar, milk, salt, and eggs into the yeast mixture until well blended.

3. *Beat:* Beat in 5 cups of flour, a little at a time, until dough is stiff and elastic. When you pull on the dough, it should return to close to the original shape and it should not stick to your hands. Add more flour, a little at a time, until the dough is elastic and does not stick to your hands. Cover dough and set aside for 1½ hours to let it rise.

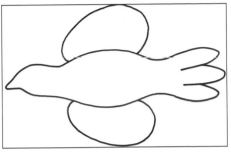

6. *Decorative detail:* Snip tail piece with scissors to create feathers. Use a toothpick to make small indentations.

7. *Cover and let rise:* Cover sculpture with cloth and let rise in a warm place for 30 minutes.

8. *Brush:* Brush dove with mixture made of 1 beaten egg and 1 tablespoon water.

9. *Bake:* Bake in a preheated 350°F oven for 30 minutes or until bread is richly browned. Let cool on pan for 10 minutes. Slip a spatula beneath dove and gently slide onto a rack to cool completely.

4. *Knead:* Lightly flour a cutting board or other work surface and knead dough for 15 minutes until smooth. Knead by pushing down on dough and away from your body, then pull dough back and repeat. Add flour as you need it to keep your hands from sticking to the dough or the dough to the work surface.

5. *Divide and shape:* Divide dough into 6 pieces of equal size. Shape each piece into a dove. Build sculpture on greased, foil-covered baking sheets. Make dove no thicker than 1 inch, or bread may crack during baking. Leave at least 2 inches of space between the birds on the baking sheets.

CHAPTER EIGHT

Flower Power

At winter's end, when the snow is melting and the trees still have bare branches, the ground starts to soften. In a few weeks, green grass and tiny plants poke up through the ground. The trees will soon burst with leaves and fill with birds. But what is this green shoot already coming up through the melting snow? It is a crocus, a flower that grows from a bulb, not very tall, with purple, white, or yellow flowers. This is only the first of many beautiful spring flowers.

Crocuses, daffodils, irises, tulips, and lilies are all flowers that grow from bulbs. If you were to dig where these flowers are planted, you would find a hard brown thing that looks like a small onion. All through the cold winter the bulb seems to be sleeping. But with spring and the softening and warming of the ground, the bulb gets warm, and tiny stems reach upward toward the sun. Once they bloom, they release a wonderful smell that is a sign of spring.

It's no wonder that spring's blooming bulbs have a place in Easter celebrations. When Jesus died he was placed in a tomb, and a large rock was rolled over the front. Lilies were brought to the tomb and set in front of the rock. Three days later, though the lilies and the rock had not been moved, when the rock was rolled away, Jesus' body was gone. Soon after, Jesus walked among his friends for the last time. From that ancient time to this, Christians of all nations have enjoyed the flowers of spring as a symbol of the Resurrection of Jesus. Bulbs sit in the ground, as if dead, and then come to life, just as Jesus was buried in the tomb and was resurrected.

Flowers such as the narcissus, tulip, and pussy willow all have special meanings at Easter. These flowers bloom in spring-

The Little Plant

In the heart of a seed
Buried deep, so deep,
A dear little plant
Lay fast asleep.

"Wake!" said the sunshine
"And creep to the light,"
"Wake!" said the voice
Of the raindrops bright.

The little plant heard,
And it rose to see
What the wonderful
Outside world might be.

— Kate L. Brown

The Flower

The stem comes up
The bud pops out
The bud opens
and the petals take a stretch—
Finally the flower has awoken
from a long winter's nap.

— Jarrett Lingelbach

Nature's Easter Music

The flowers from the earth have arisen,
They are singing their Easter-song;
Up the valleys and over the hillsides
They come, an unnumbered throng.

Oh, listen! The wild-flowers are singing
Their beautiful songs without words!

— Lucy Larcom

The Flower Garden

This is not father's garden
This is not mother's garden
Mine and yours, everybody's
This little garden belongs to everyone

— Kelsang Shakya

time, and people use them to make their homes pretty for the holiday. But the most popular Easter flower is the lily.

Greek mythology says that the lily first sprang from the milk of Hera, the wife of Zeus. Semitic legend claims that the lily sprang from the tear of Eve when she was expelled from the Garden of Eden. She cried as she left the garden, and wherever her tears fell, a lily grew.

Lilies grew in Jerusalem, or the Holy Land, and carvings of them adorned the Temple. The Bible says that Jesus loved the lilies. There are many other Bible stories about the lily. Mary, the mother of Jesus, on her way to the temple, picked a yellow lily, and when she clutched it to her breast, it turned a pure bright white. For this reason the lily is sometimes called the "Madonna Lily." In paintings of Mary, you will often see a lily in her hand or in a pretty vase nearby.

Naturally, people thought this must be a very powerful flower—perhaps a little magical, too. Old medical practices said that lily ointments and creams would clear the skin and even make cuts and bruises go away.

Strangely enough, the shiny white flower we call an Easter lily wasn't always so closely associated with springtime. The Easter lily was brought from islands in the Pacific Ocean, where the seasons are quite different from ours and the lily flowers all year long. Here it doesn't naturally bloom in the spring, but has to be helped by keeping its bulb at the right temperature and giving it the right amount of water.

Easter flowers bring reassurance that spring will come again after a cold, bleak winter. Life keeps going and going, coming anew year after year. Celebrating the coming of spring with beautiful flowers has become a familiar part of Easter.

The crocus, an early spring flower, is appreciated for more than just its beauty. This flower is the source of saffron, a spice, as well as dye, scent, and even medication. It used to be said that having saffron was as good as having gold or money, for it is very useful.

People make a potion from lilies by mixing the flowers with honey. Then they rub the potion on their skin to make it soft. One recipe calls for 3,000 flowers!

In the seventeenth century, the Dutch, French, and English were wild for tulips. People began to bid against each other for the purchase of the lovely flowers. The prices went up and up, until the highest recorded purchase was for three tulips sold at $30,000!

Antipasto Flowers

In Italian, *antipasto* means "before the pasta." This recipe creates flowers out of different vegetables and cheese. This antipasto makes a plate full of powerful flowers.

INGREDIENTS FOR FLOWERS

Celery, cut into 6 inch pieces

Green, red, and yellow peppers, cut into ¼ x 3 inch strips

Cauliflower, cut into 2 inch florets

Carrots, peeled and cut into ½ x 3 inch strips

Radishes, cut into ¼ inch thick rounds

Nut cups

Cheddar cheese, cut into ¼ inch thick slices

Cherry tomatoes, cut in half

Cream cheese

Alfalfa sprouts

INGREDIENTS FOR 1 CUP AVOCADO DRESSING

1 avocado

½ cup sour cream

2 tablespoons milk

1 tablespoon lemon juice

1. Arrange vegetables and cheese on large white platter in flower designs. Use celery for flower stems; green pepper for leaves; red pepper, yellow pepper, cauliflower, carrots, or cheddar cheese for flower petals; radishes, nut cups (filled with dip), or cherry tomatoes for flower centers. When you have the designs you like, secure by spreading a little cream cheese on the back of the vegetable pieces.

2. Arrange alfalfa sprouts at the base of the flowers to look like grass, and place platter in refrigerator while you make the dip.

3. For dip, peel and seed avocado and mash with a fork. Mix avocado, sour cream, milk, and lemon juice until creamy. Spoon into nut cups, and add to flower arrangement.

4. For dip, peel and seed avocado and mash with a fork. Mix avocado, sour cream, milk, and lemon juice until creamy. Spoon into nut cups, and add to flower arrangement.

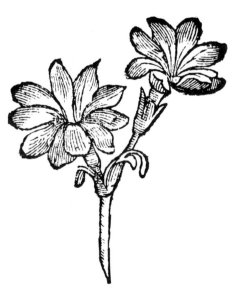

The Magic Easter Lily

BY MARY ROBINSON

Lenny had a big problem. He couldn't keep his room clean. He tried, but somehow clothes swam across the floor, baseball cards spilled over the shelves, and toys jumped off every surface. Worst of all, he couldn't find his baseball glove.

He ran to the kitchen. His parents were drinking tea and reading the newspaper.

"Baseball practice is in an hour and I can't find my glove. Will you help me?"

"Have you tried cleaning your room?" asked his mom.

"I will. As soon as I get home from practice."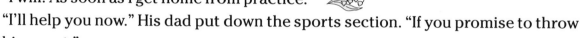

"I'll help you now." His dad put down the sports section. "If you promise to throw some things out."

"I can't promise that, Dad. I have to get organized first."

"That's right, Lenny, but time is going by."

"I know," Lenny said. "Baseball practice is in an hour."

"Clean one corner of your room," said his dad. "And I'll drive you to the field."

"But my glove," protested Lenny.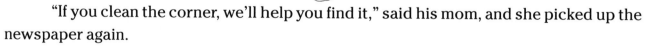

"If you clean the corner, we'll help you find it," said his mom, and she picked up the newspaper again.

That sounded fair to Lenny. He returned to his room and started cleaning the corner beside the door. He picked up clothes, put away toys, and went through boxes of old treasures. He found his bottle cap collection, then his used golf ball collection, and even his seashell collection from two summers ago.

As Lenny set out these long-lost collections, he shoved toys and clothes aside to make room for them. He didn't notice that the pile behind him was getting bigger and bigger. When he emptied the last box, he discovered the pile blocked the door and he couldn't open it wide enough to get out.

"Hey, Mom! Dad! Help! I'm trapped!"

"I don't believe it," said his dad through the door. "I thought you were cleaning up."

"I was but—but—"

"Stand back," said his dad.

His dad pushed the door with his shoulder and shoved his way into the room. "You need to get organized, son."

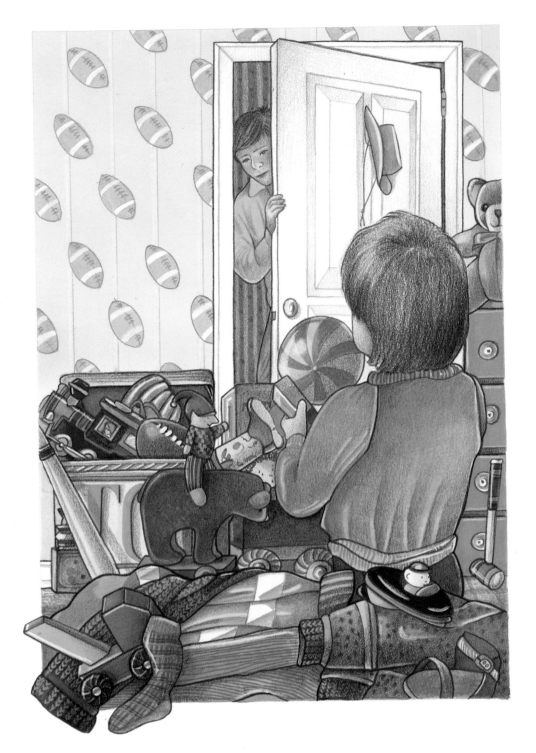

"I know, Dad. I'm trying. See the corner?"

Lenny's dad frowned, but agreed the corner was clean. Then he searched and found Lenny's glove under a sweatshirt in back of the sports equipment basket.

On the way to the field, his dad said, "You tried and that's what counts. But you need a plan. Make your room into a grid like your battleship game. You be the torpedo that wipes out the mess in a part of the grid each day."

"Great," said Lenny. "I like that idea. I'll make a grid tonight."

Lenny cleaned a part of the room each day. But somehow by Sunday it was worse.

His dad shook his head. "Maybe you need a deadline."

"That sounds good to me," said Lenny. "Give me a deadline."

"Hmmm," said his dad. "When was the last time your room was totally clean?"

"Last Easter when Grandma helped me."

"Well, Easter's three weeks from today. Let's make the deadline Easter."

"Okay, it's a deal," said Lenny.

"Deadlines have consequences if you don't meet them," said his mom. "If your room isn't clean by Easter, then the Easter Bunny isn't going to leave you anything."

"Wait a minute. That's not fair," protested Lenny. He liked getting an Easter basket filled with his favorite candies.

"Oh, yes it is," said his dad, firmly but kindly. "Don't forget: we're on your side. We think you can do it."

"Okay, I'll give it my best," Lenny agreed reluctantly.

Lenny went out on the front steps to figure out what he could do about this terrible situation. He really wanted to get an Easter basket and all the special Easter goodies. But how was he going to clean his room?

While he was considering pushing everything into the closet, Lenny heard, "Hey, kid. Want to buy a magic Easter lily? It lives forever and you don't have to water it."

There in front of him was a short wiry man with bushy eyebrows, holding a clay pot.

"That's just a pot of dirt," said Lenny.

"Ah, but inside the dirt is the bulb of a lily. And by Easter this lily will be so beautiful and so magical, you won't believe what will happen."

"I don't think my parents would be happy about my talking to you."

The man stepped back to the sidewalk and said, "Don't worry. I just want to sell you this lily. I promise that when it blossoms something magical will happen."

Lenny couldn't resist, so he bought the lily with the money he'd saved from his allowance. Then he carried it to the kitchen to show his parents.

"It's a magic lily!" He told them what the man promised.

"Oh Lenny," said his mom. "It looks like just a pot of dirt."

His dad shook his head. "Well, let's be positive. Take the pot to your room and we'll see what happens. While you're waiting, clean your room."

It took Lenny two minutes to wade through the mess on the floor of his room to the window. He put the pot on the window sill and leaned against his bed. "Please be magical," he whispered to the lily.

Lenny checked the pot every day, but nothing appeared in the dirt. He brought the lily pot to show-and-tell at school and repeated what the short wiry man with bushy eyebrows had said. Only a few kids, and not even all his friends, said they believed there was a lily in the pot.

The second Sunday before Easter, Lenny was ready to give up and throw the pot out. But on Monday morning the pot sprouted a stalk.

"Wow!" yelled Lenny. "I'm going to have a lily."

"That's wonderful!" exclaimed his dad.

"The stalk is a good sign but let's wait and see," said his mom.

Lenny waited and Lenny watched. Every day the stalk grew taller. And every day

Lenny stopped playing with his friends a little earlier than the day before. He came home to watch his lily grow. He walked to the window so often, that soon there was a wide clear path across the room.

On Friday a bud appeared. Lenny cleared off the rest of the window sill. He was tired of standing up to watch his lily, so he cleaned off his bed and sat down. He even came home right after school to measure the growth of the stalk and the bud. He cleaned off his desk so he could make a chart. Then he wanted to put the chart on the wall. But before he could hang it, he had to clear a path to the wall.

During the week before Easter, Lenny's friends begged to see what was happening with the lily. He invited his best friend over first, then other friends. And as more kids came over, Lenny had to clear a bigger and bigger space for them to fit into his room.

Then on Saturday morning Lenny woke up to a wonderful smell. He opened his eyes to see that his Easter lily had sprouted a bloom. The lily was the most beautiful flower Lenny had ever seen. It was so beautiful he wanted the room to be clean.

He was cleaning and chanting, "It's a lily. It's a lily," when his dad and mom came in.

"That Easter lily is lovely," exclaimed his mom. "And so is this room!"

His dad gave Lenny a wonderful bear hug and shouted, "I knew you could do it, son. This room looks great. Just great!"

Lenny lifted the lily. "Here, Mom, this is for you. It really is a magic lily. You can see how it helped me." He grinned. There was nothing left to pick up in his room. And he couldn't believe it but—he liked it that way.

Foam Lily

There are many wonderful spring flowers. The lily is the one most closely associated with Easter. There are other lilies that bloom in spring besides the Easter lily. One of these is the calla lily, which is also called the "Lily of the Nile." The word *calla* means "beautiful."

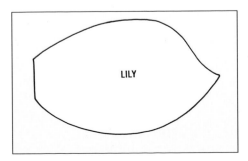

MATERIALS

Wire cutters

1 wire hanger

1 12 x 18-inch sheet each yellow, white, and green foam craft

Needle

Yellow thread

Yellow glass beads

White glue

Yellow glitter

Thin wire

Glue gun and glue (use a cool glue gun or get help using a hot one)

1 24 x 20-inch sheet green tissue paper, cut in 2-inch strips

STEPS

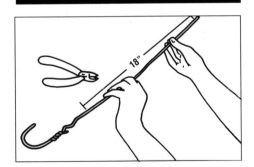

1. *Cut hanger:* With the wire cutters, cut the hanger as shown and straighten 18 inches of it. Leave the hook part of hanger on as a handle. You will cut this off later.

7. *Wrap:* Tightly wrap the remainder of the stem with green tissue. (This will give a green background in case there are any gaps in the green foam.)

8. *Cut:* Cut green foam into 3 ½-x-18-inch pieces. Angle cut the ends. Remove thin wire from base of white lily.

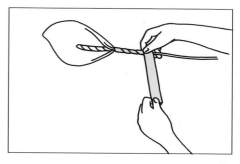

9. *Secure and wrap:* Take your time and secure the top of green foam to the base of the flower at the back by using the glue gun. Glue green foam strip every 2 inches and wrap down the wire. Pull the foam slightly to make a tight wrap. When the first strip of green is finished, glue on a new one where the first one stops.

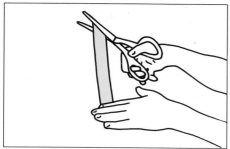

2. *Cut foam:* Cut a ½ x 18-inch strip of yellow foam. Cut the ends at an angle as shown.

3. *Sew:* With needle and thread, sew beads randomly on one side of the yellow strip.

down at an angle as you go. Glue about every inch. The yellow should cover 4 inches of the top end of the wire.

5. *Add glitter:* Spread white glue on the 4-inch yellow end. Roll in glitter and let dry.

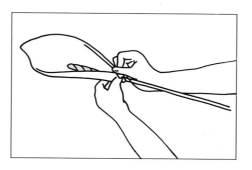

6. *Cut and glue:* Cut a white lily in shape shown. Dot glue at the base of the flower. Wrap the flower at the bottom of the yellow center, turning the bottom of the white foam back onto itself. Secure with the thin wire. Wire will be removed when the glue is set.

10. *Hold and remove:* Wrap the thin wire around the green foam to hold it down while glue sets. Remove thin wire when glue has dried.

11. *Cut wire:* Have an adult help you cut off the hook part of hanger with wire cutters.

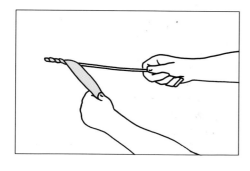

4. *Glue:* Carefully wrap the yellow strip around the end of the straightened hanger, pulling